"My, my," he murmured. "The lady's getting frisky."

Daringly, she nibbled his finger before releasing his hand. Marta wasn't sure where she had found the nerve. She grinned. "You taste pretty good."

"How about you?" Before Marta could react, Derek leaned toward her and grazed the corner of her mouth with his lips.

The quick kiss sent liquid pleasure through her. She tried not to show any reaction as he withdrew, but she wanted more. "No wonder they call you Sergeant Hit-and-Run."

"Too fast?" he enquired.

"The breeze gave me a chill."

Dear Reader,

I've always loved Cinderella stories, whether in a fairy-tale format or applied to a realistic setting and characters. With new twists and genuine emotion, the enchantment never wanes.

Even after writing more than seventy novels, I still can't explain where characters come from or how they take on lives of their own. Marta arrived in my imagination first, a feisty young woman who survived near-fatal injuries and other hardships without relinquishing her dreams. As the man she fell in love with, Derek fascinated me with his depths and his painful secret.

Hope you enjoy reading their tale as much as I enjoyed writing it!

Best,

Jacqueline Diamond

TWIN SURPRISE
Jacqueline Diamond

TORONTO • NEW YORK • LONDON
AMSTERDAM • PARIS • SYDNEY • HAMBURG
STOCKHOLM • ATHENS • TOKYO • MILAN • MADRID
PRAGUE • WARSAW • BUDAPEST • AUCKLAND

ISBN-13: 978-0-373-75181-5
ISBN-10:   0-373-75181-8

TWIN SURPRISE

ABOUT THE AUTHOR

A former Associated Press reporter, Jacqueline Diamond has written more than seventy novels and received a Career Achievement Award from *Romantic Times BOOKreviews*. Jackie lives in Southern California with her husband, two sons and two cats. You can e-mail her at jdiamondfriends@aol.com or visit her Web site at www.jacquelinediamond.com.

Books by Jacqueline Diamond

HARLEQUIN AMERICAN ROMANCE

*Downhome Doctors

Don't miss any of our special offers. Write to us at the following address for information on our newest releases.

Harlequin Reader Service
U.S.: 3010 Walden Ave., P.O. Box 1325, Buffalo, NY 14269
Canadian: P.O. Box 609, Fort Erie, Ont. L2A 5X3

To Kurt, my wonderfully supportive husband.

Chapter One

If she ever had a chance at a storybook wedding, Marta Lawson thought, she'd choose one just like this: a beautiful Saturday in October, the church filling with friends and family and, waiting at the altar, a man too special for words.

Well, best not to think about that last part.

She refocused on the decorations she'd helped select. Amid the blue-and-white flower arrangements, porcelain-doll faces peered out of frosty lace cascades like princesses from another world. In the foyer, a doll wearing a replica of the bridal gown sat on a tabletop beside the guest book.

The bride—Marta's cousin Connie—had devised additional charming touches: china figurines arranged here and there amid miniature bouquets, and prisms by the windows that split the light into shimmering colors. Connie's owning two boutiques and a hospital gift concession gave her and Marta, the maid of honor, a definite edge when it came to finding such treasures. Marta, in fact, managed the concession, located in the Mesa View Medical Center in Villazon, California. She took pride in ferreting out appealing items from catalogs and Internet sites.

"Connie sure did a number on this place," said bridesmaid Rachel McKenzie, who at five foot eleven towered over the diminutive Marta. The two stood in the otherwise empty vestibule, sneaking peeks into the sanctuary. At any minute, the photo-taking of the bride with her parents would finish and the ceremony could begin.

Mercifully, Connie had allowed her two attendants to wear blue dresses instead of her original choice, shell pink, which hadn't suited Rachel at all. Nevertheless, the taller bridesmaid kept fidgeting as if she couldn't wait to change into her usual attire: police uniform and boots. As for Marta, her shorter stature wasn't all the guests might notice. Despite her best efforts, her tendrils of light brown, shoulder-length hair didn't entirely hide the scars from a near-fatal car crash nearly a dozen years ago, and the walk down the aisle would inevitably expose her limp.

But to be able to walk at all was a blessing. And her scars…well, what did a few blemishes matter in the wake of near tragedy?

Okay, in one respect they *did* matter. If Marta were pretty and graceful, the best man, Sergeant Derek Reed, might see her as something more than a buddy.

But she wouldn't like that, not really. At the police department, Derek had a reputation as a playboy. And at the hospital, where he conducted weekly crime-prevention seminars, the nurses who dropped into Marta's shop referred to him as Sergeant Hit-and-Run.

Wistfully, she gazed past the rows of guests, who included fellow employees, police colleagues of the groom's and a sprinkling of other friends and relatives. Near the altar, her gaze riveted on the masculine figure poised beside the groom.

Derek in a tuxedo constituted overkill: a well-toned body, thick blond hair and dark eyes that surveyed the scene with deceptive laziness. He drew feminine interest as easily as he breathed.

Not only was he a close friend of Connie's husband-to-be, Detective Hale Crandall, but both men had originally entered Marta's circle of friends several years ago as buddies of

Connie's first husband, Sergeant—now Lieutenant—Joel Simmons. During her cousin's troubled early marriage and the years following the divorce, Marta had succeeded in banishing the unattainable Derek to the periphery of her thoughts.

Then, nearly a year ago, the police chief had appointed him to the position of community relations and public information officer. His tasks included finessing the questions of reporters intent on rehashing old police department scandals, a good post for such an articulate man.

His duties also included coordinating a public service program to detect and prevent crimes ranging from child neglect to prescription-drug abuse. In that capacity, he visited the hospital every Thursday morning for staff meetings.

To the best of Marta's knowledge, he'd had two girlfriends during this period, neither of whom had lasted more than a few months. There'd also been several flirtations, most—in her observation—instigated by the women.

When he arrived for the meetings, Derek had formed the habit of stopping in to purchase a candy bar and swap jokes with Marta. She searched the Internet for funny items to inspire his wonderful deep laughter.

How exhausting to feel eager anticipation each time he approached and rueful disappointment when he left! Maybe if he fell in love with someone, she'd finally see what a hopeless case she was and get over him.

Marta sighed. When Rachel quirked an eyebrow, she covered her feelings by gesturing toward the sanctuary. "Doesn't everyone look great all dressed up?"

"I think Skip needs to go to the bathroom," replied the pragmatic Rachel, indicating the seven-year-old ring bearer. The former foster child, whom the bride and groom were adopting, bounced from one foot to the other.

"He's just excited," Marta said.

"Somebody ought to calm him down before he ricochets off the wall," Rachel responded.

Hale must have entertained similar thoughts, because he aimed a couple of mock punches at his son-to-be. The two tussled playfully before settling into their proper positions once more.

Marta saw Derek give a half smile. Once the most outgoing in a highly sociable group of police officers, he'd begun holding himself apart in recent months. At least, he'd seemed that way to Marta; no one else had commented on the change. Perhaps he'd always maintained a certain reserve and she simply hadn't noticed.

The swish of fabric drew the bridesmaids' attention toward the hall. Connie had arrived with her mother and father in tow. Her stepmother had taken a seat earlier.

Marta's beautiful blond cousin had always been a draw for men. Today, in a sleek silk gown, a wreath of flowers and a glow of happiness, she looked magnificent.

She and Hale were perfect for each other, although they'd taken a long while to discover that. With Connie's sharp tongue and Hale's talent for provoking her, the two next-door neighbors had carried on a friendly feud for years.

They'd recognized their mutual attraction at last, becoming the second new couple among Marta's tight-knit circle. Only five months ago, Rachel and pediatrician Russ McKenzie had exchanged vows at this same altar. Rachel, who'd expected to be the last of the trio to marry, used to joke that she'd probably have to arrest the guy first, and in fact had mistaken Russ for a suspect when they initially met. He still teased her about handcuffing him.

To Marta, marriage seemed a distant and receding dream. Fortunately, she had other goals. After putting her education on hold during her rehabilitation, she'd finally saved enough money to take an evening class at a nearby university and planned to sign up for two classes next semester. Eventually she'd be a teacher, as she'd always wanted.

So she tried not to envy her cousin that beatific expression or the love that awaited her at the end of the aisle. Marta was genuinely glad for Connie. She also relished the temporary peace between her high-strung aunt Anna and strong-willed uncle Jim, ex-spouses who'd set aside their differences to walk their daughter down the aisle. In their late fifties, both retained more than a little of the good looks and natural elegance that had once made them a dazzling couple.

"We better line up, huh?" Rachel scooted to the sanctuary entrance and raised her bouquet. Marta took a position behind her.

"Remember not to gallop!" Anna warned.

"How about a fast trot?" Rachel, famous for her long legs and rapid pace, grinned at the group. "Don't tell me you all forgot your roller skates!"

The bride's laughter softened her mother's frown. "Skip would get a kick out of that," Anna conceded. Although not the grandmotherly type, she'd developed a fondness for her new grandson.

In the sanctuary, the organist shifted into a march. "Everyone ready?" asked Uncle Jim.

"Ready as we'll ever be," Rachel rejoined.

"Go! Go!" urged Aunt Anna.

Rachel began at a stately pace, forgetting herself only so far as to wave the bouquet at her husband and young stepdaughter, Lauren. Unfortunately, however, she couldn't contain herself for more than a few yards, and soon shifted into second gear, then third.

The unfortunate result was that, when Rachel reached the altar, Marta still faced a long stretch of aisle. She felt a hundred or so pairs of eyes absorbing the unevenness of her gait. And surely everyone noticed that one of her pumps had a built-up sole to compensate for the length that leg had lost.

Marta kept her chin up. When she felt a pinch of pain in her hip, she did her best to hide it.

Ahead, Derek lifted one eyebrow sympathetically. He

really had wonderful brows: thick, with an arch on the right side that did a splendid job of expressing skepticism or shared humor, as now. His warmth put the whole situation into perspective and helped dissipate her awkwardness.

With relief, Marta reached the front and assumed her place. As the music soared and all faces turned toward the head of the aisle, she whispered to Rachel, "Bouquet!"

Her fellow bridesmaid jerked the drooping flowers into place. "Thanks," she murmured. "And sorry about my gallop."

To the strains of "Here Comes the Bride," Connie glided into view. Hale practically levitated with joy. The guy had been in love with Connie for years, Marta suspected, perhaps even before her divorce. Now he no longer had to conceal his feelings.

The whole church pulsed with good wishes. What more could a person ask than to be surrounded by the people she loved? Being part of this event felt almost like having a wedding of her own, Marta thought. She really was a lucky person in more ways than she could count.

AT YESTERDAY'S REHEARSAL, Derek hadn't taken much notice of the instructions beyond his duties during the wedding ceremony. He must have missed the part about standing in a receiving line at the reception. What fiend had devised this method of torture? he wondered as the umpteenth guest shuffled by en route to the nuptial couple.

His smile felt frozen in place. His back ached and his knee was bothering him. He'd identified strongly with Marta during her brave trek down the aisle.

Despite the discomfort, he was glad for Hale, who deserved this happiness. And grateful for the scents emanating from the buffet set up here in the Villa Inn ballroom. Now, when the heck would he and everybody else in this receiving line get a chance to sample that cuisine?

Also, despite his stiffness, the rhythms thrumming from the band made him feel more like twenty-five than thirty-five.

Speaking of which, he'd give a lot to be twenty-five again, or even thirty. He'd had no idea those were the good old days. Ignorance really *had* been bliss.

During a lull between handshaking while the guests bunched at one end of the line, he turned to Marta beside him. Looming nearly a foot taller, Derek enjoyed an excellent view of the part in her hair and the cute curve of her nose.

"Who are all these people?" he asked rhetorically.

Her heart-shaped face tilted toward him as she indicated a distinguished older woman teaching Skip a dance move on the otherwise empty floor. "Well, that's Yolanda Rios. She and I founded the homework center." Staffed by volunteers, the program provided tutoring for many of Villazon's struggling young students.

Marta could be such an innocent, Derek reflected. "I'd be a failure at community relations if I weren't on hugging terms with Yolanda." He was about to explain that he hadn't expected an answer to his question when he saw someone who *did* arouse his curiosity. "Who's that lady dripping with diamonds?"

In her mid-forties and smartly dressed, the woman hung on the arm of a sixtyish man. Her expensive jewelry and trendy hairstyle reeked of money. Not exactly the type of woman one met often in blue-collar Villazon, a town on the eastern edge of Los Angeles County, unfashionably far from Beverly Hills and Newport Beach.

"That's my stepmother, Bryn," Marta said, to his astonishment. "Connie refers to her as Aunt Bling, but don't you dare."

This woman lived in high style while her stepdaughter pinched pennies? Derek had heard from friends about Marta's struggles to support herself during and after rehab. Still, perhaps Bryn had earned her money. "What kind of work does she do?"

"She quit her secretarial job when she married Dad."

"Is she an heiress?"

"Don't believe so."

Derek glared at the woman. Instinctively, feeling a bit off balance, he clamped a hand onto Marta's shoulder to brace himself. "Sorry." Embarrassed by his clumsiness, he straightened.

"Why? It's not every day I get groped by a hunk," she shot back.

"If anybody gropes you, let me know and I'll deal with him," Derek growled with pretended ferocity. Leaning down, he caught a whiff of Marta's springlike scent and nearly planted a kiss on the tip of her nose.

Crazy notion. He liked Marta, but that was the extent of his feelings.

Before he could return to the subject of her stepmother and the besotted bald man who must be her father, the line of guests broke its gridlock and surged toward them. More out-thrust hands to shake, more pleasantries to exchange.

Across the ballroom, the band segued from a rock number to a Latin beat. Man, Derek loved to dance. Considering his balance problems, he probably ought to give it up, but not yet. They'd be through receiving guests any minute now, anyway.

"You're wiggling," Marta said.

His hips *were* swaying. "How's your mambo?"

"That beat isn't a mambo," she pointed out. "And with one leg shorter than the other, I look weird on the dance floor."

He appreciated Marta's candor. Still, she wasn't the only one with limitations. "Well, my leg's a little stiff from exercising, but I refuse to let that stop me. Why don't we go out there and tackle that Latin thing."

Marta shook her head. "I've staggered around in public enough for one day." However, the rhythmic twitch of her shoulders spoke more loudly than her protests.

"No one's watching." Derek gripped her waist and cradled her hand in his. "Let's tango our way over there, Cinderella."

She was so small and light he could have picked her up and

carried her to the dance floor, except that he'd probably trip. And she might kick him in the shins for his efforts.

She escaped his grasp. "Not in front of everyone! And why'd you call me Cinderella?"

Derek grinned. "Because you have a wicked stepmother."

Her green eyes sparkled. "But no stepsisters. Or brothers."

"The comparison still applies." He'd heard the story in bits and pieces. "She persuaded your father to cut you off after they married, right?"

"No," Marta replied. "When I turned twenty-one, he felt that since I wasn't a dependent anymore, state aid should pay for my rehab."

"Great move, leaving his daughter to fend for herself." Derek frowned at this Aunt Bling, who remained oblivious. "Meanwhile his new wife is wearing his bank account on her earlobes."

Marta looked at him in a manner that Derek would have considered amusing had not his tiny antagonist appeared so earnest. "It's Dad's hard-earned money. I'm just glad he met a woman who makes him happy. He suffered a lot after my mom died."

She had an endearingly warm heart even toward those who'd treated her badly, which made Derek angry on her behalf. Still, he had to admit, he'd sometimes been accused of hard-heartedness himself. He always told women in advance that he wasn't the settling-down type. If they chose to ignore the warning, he couldn't be held responsible.

Marta, however, fell into the category of people under Derek's protection. Or, at least, of people he'd protect if they required it.

"You should stand up to your father," he persisted. "That necklace she's sporting could buy you a master's degree."

Marta bristled. "I'm standing up to *you*. Back off, buster."

"Yes, ma'am!" He took her words literally, executing a brief retreat and a bow. Then he caught her again and whirled her toward the dance floor. "This time I'm not taking no for an answer."

Apparently Marta decided to relax and enjoy the moment. Her whole being seemed to respond to the catchy music as they navigated between tables toward the dance floor. And for once, his body cooperated, as well.

They shimmied past Lois Lamont, the chief's secretary, who favored them with a thumbs-up. Derek responded with a wink.

When Marta chuckled at his clowning, her energy gave him a lift. At that moment, he actually felt twenty-five again.

They reached the dance floor as the band shifted into another catchy tune. Despite a few missteps, the two of them finished the number in fine form.

Both were flushed with their efforts. Marta exuded a natural appeal that made Derek wonder why the other men in the room hadn't swarmed over to demand the next turn.

He eased her off the dance floor. "What do you say we hit the buffet?"

"Sure. I'm starving."

They filled their plates with the finger foods and browsed the tables in their roles as best man and maid of honor. Derek traded quips with his former supervisor in the detective bureau, Captain Frank Ferguson, who sat with Chief Will Lyons and retired sergeant Mack Crandall, Hale's father.

At another table, Marta introduced several of Connie's employees, including an attractive twenty-year-old with long brown hair who studied him with interest. A pretty girl, but too young to interest Derek.

Finally the two of them settled near the newlyweds. Hale appeared in his element as host of a large party, and Connie seemed more relaxed than she'd been in ages. She didn't so much as frown when her ex-husband, Joel, swung into a chair beside her.

The once-feuding exes had achieved détente a few months earlier, to everyone's relief. Derek didn't understand the point of such squabbling. Once the excitement went out of a relationship, people ought to say farewell and move on.

"Let's see that ring," Joel teased. "I'll bet it's not half as nice as the one I bought you."

Connie displayed her fingers gracefully. To Derek, the rock looked big enough to decimate a guy's life savings.

"Cost me a bundle," Hale confirmed heartily. "Worth every penny."

"Hey, I liked the one Joel bought her," Rachel chipped in from further down the table. She'd borrowed that ring when first engaged to her husband.

"*Rachel* has good taste," Joel responded. "And my sister's thrilled that you gave her the old ring. Nice gesture, Connie."

"She mentioned that she lost her wedding ring on vacation this summer," the bride explained.

All this camaraderie would once have filled Derek with a sense of belonging. On entering police work, he'd felt as if were joining a real family, one that suited him a lot better than the one into which he'd been born. Yet today, as it had many other days in the past year, the banter flowed around him at a distance, an invisible wall muting sounds and blurring images.

Strange how just a few minutes in a doctor's office could change a guy's perspective.

It had also altered his career. As soon as he'd informed Human Resources of the diagnosis, the powers that be had stuck Derek in a front-office job requiring less physical exertion. Derek would rather face a weekly shoot-out than shuffle paper, but his friends, unaware of the true circumstances, considered this a promotion.

He abandoned his ruminations as Yolanda Rios arrived. "Aha, the two people I most want to talk to," she declared, pinning him and Marta with her gaze.

"A pleasure to see you, Yolanda." He rose and fetched an extra chair. Their companions shifted to clear space.

"Thanks. I've got an idea and I'd appreciate feedback from all of you." The widow pushed her glasses higher on the bridge of her nose. "And don't you go anywhere, Joel Simmons!"

The lieutenant paused halfway to his feet and sat down again as if he were still a student in Yolanda's high-school history class. "I was going to refill your glass of punch."

"Thanks, but it can wait." She folded her hands on the table.

"What's up?" Marta asked.

Yolanda included them all in her gaze. "To start with, although I hate to break the news on such a festive occasion, the city's cut funding for Villa Corazon." Villa Corazon was the name of the homework center. It meant House of the Heart in Spanish and was a play on its location in the town of Villazon.

"That's outrageous!" Connie radiated indignation. "If you need me to organize a protest, I'd be glad to."

The older woman shook her head. "If we demand a bigger share of a shrinking budget, that puts us in competition with other worthwhile programs. I favor a more proactive approach."

Marta regarded Yolanda expectantly. The two spent a lot of hours together at the center, Derek assumed, but she didn't appear to know what was coming. "What do you have in mind?"

"A fund-raiser." With all attention fixed on her, she announced, "I propose we hold a bachelor auction. There's no shortage of attractive males in town or generous and assertive women."

Startled expressions and a few chuckles greeted this statement. "Wild!" Rachel said. "I'd go for that. If I was single, I mean."

"Why not?" Hale agreed. "A romantic night on the town with your favorite hottie. Not me, of course."

"Isn't that kind of…old-fashioned?" Derek refused to disclose his personal reservations about parading in front of a group. Surely the center could find a more dignified means of raising money.

Joel let out a hoot. "I should think you'd be the first to volunteer!"

"You're an excellent prospect also, Lieutenant Simmons," Yolanda observed.

"I'm divorced, not a bachelor," he declared. He hadn't expected to get drafted, apparently.

"If she excludes divorced men, she'd have to rule out two-thirds of her prospects," Hale countered. "Don't tell me you're chicken."

"Heck, no." Joel appeared to be searching frantically for an escape route. "Tell you what—I'll emcee the darned thing."

"Hale can tackle that duty, since he's married." Yolanda looked at the groom. "All right?"

"Glad to," he said.

"Lieutenant, can I count you in?" Yolanda prompted.

Joel yielded to the inevitable. "Fine. I'll be glad to go on the block for charity."

The older woman turned to Derek. "As will, I presume, the city's community relations officer."

She'd cornered him, Derek thought. The PD could use positive ink for a change. Besides, a refusal would invite questions Derek preferred to avoid.

"I was about to offer my services," he responded dryly. "I enjoy meeting new ladies."

"You mean new victims?" Rachel teased.

"Anyone who bids for him hardly qualifies as a victim," Marta responded loyally.

"Exactly." Derek hoped the easy response hid his qualms.

More voices joined in, adding to the roster. Rachel's husband mentioned an old friend, a child psychologist named Mike Federov. Hale listed a couple of other officers and suggested contacting the fire department.

The conversation drifted to the terms of the auction purchase. An afternoon or evening—minimum three hours—that might range from a lavish date to a simple outing. Whatever suited the bidder and biddee, with the man paying the cost of the date.

The whole thing sounded very civilized, except that as more men stopped by and offered their names, Derek detected a competitive mood building. Joel went so far as to recommend they all wear swim trunks.

Yolanda nixed the idea. "We're a children's center. Although I doubt there'll be kids at this event, I'd like to keep things respectable."

"I hope that doesn't preclude a little showing off to get the highest bid of the night." Joel shot a challenging look at Derek. "Not that I expect much competition."

Rachel whistled her approval. "That sounds like a dare."

Derek shrugged. "He's deluded."

Marta, he noticed, looked wistful. Now, what was that about?

"Would jeans and a T-shirt be too casual?" he asked her.

She studied him thoughtfully. "How about your uniform? Women love a man in uniform."

"The chief might not go for that," Hale interposed. "Especially if the *Villazon Voice* takes photos of our guys onstage."

Derek shrugged. "Either a suit or jeans will be fine."

"Then I'm definitely leaving you in the dust," Joel replied. "I'm thinking about exercise shorts and a mesh shirt."

Connie rolled her eyes. Rachel uttered a woo-woo noise.

"I'd like to schedule this a couple of weeks from now, toward the end of October," Yolanda said. "Before people spend all their money on the holidays."

"Besides, what a great gift for the single gal on your list," put in Rachel's husband, Russ.

"I'm betting plenty of single gals will buy *themselves* a gift that night," Connie mused. "Derek, you should charm Tracy Johnson into bidding on you and writing a story. She owes the department a little boost." Tracy, editor and reporter for the weekly *Voice*, had long been one of the police department's biggest gadflies.

"The chief would love reading a detailed front-page account of Derek's shortcomings," Joel joked.

"If she wrote an article about spending the night with me, she'd have to write a book," Derek responded.

A chorus of good-natured catcalls greeted this boast. Although pleased at scoring points, in truth Derek loathed the prospect of being bid on like a prize bull. Worse, of risking an awkward stumble in front of an audience.

Well, he'd bluff his way through the ordeal. And who knew? Maybe he'd find the woman of his dreams.

But she'd be temporary. Because these days, that was all he wanted or needed.

Chapter Two

Marta wasn't certain the Halloween costumes had been a good idea. Sure, they looked creative and colorful in catalogs, but that didn't mean they'd sell in a hospital gift shop, especially since she'd unthinkingly assumed staff members would be among the main purchasers.

She'd argued back and forth with herself before ordering a small selection. On the one hand, patients arriving for major surgery might not appreciate seeing admitting clerks garbed as princesses or superheroes. Plus, the garments couldn't be sterilized. On the other hand, surely the denizens of the children's floor and the maternity ward deserved a little fun.

Ultimately, the employees would make their own decision. She'd already received an okay from the administrator.

With the lobby nearly empty on Thursday morning a week after the wedding, she used the time to snap a portable trellis-type support into place near the front of the shop. Perched on a stepstool equipped with side rails, Marta hoisted an array of capes and tunics into place.

She was almost finished when she spotted Elise Masterson striding out of an elevator. Even a uniform couldn't hide the patrolwoman's feminine shape, and scraping her honey-blond hair into a bun barely muted the effect of her attractive features. Only her habitual scowl managed to quell the interested glance an orderly aimed in her direction.

Although Elise radiated *Leave me alone!* vibes, men continued to hit on her. Two years ago, she'd fended off the advances of then police chief Vince Borrego. Elise's formal complaint had sparked an investigation that led to the chief's early retirement and pitted several of the senior officers against her. Joel and Hale, who'd testified on her behalf, had also taken heat. The damage inflicted on the department's reputation by that incident, as well as another involving prisoner abuse, still hadn't entirely healed.

Marta was distressed to observe scrapes on the officer's cheek and arms. "What happened to you?" she asked when Elise approached.

"Grabbed a toddler off a second-floor balcony and fell onto a rosebush. The nurse gave me a tetanus shot. The kid's fine, by the way." The officer paused to examine the costume display. "Do you honestly expect to sell these?"

"Sure." Marta refused to let the other woman's negativity discourage her. "Can I interest you in a set of fairy wings?"

"As if I'd be caught dead in getup like that!" Elise snorted.

"Seriously, we should all wear costumes tomorrow night at the auction. I mean, Halloween *is* next week." As volunteers at Villa Corazon, Elise and Marta had offered to assist at the auction, for which they expected a capacity crowd. "They'd add to the festive air."

"I'll be there to help direct traffic, not put on a show" came the dour response. "Speaking of shows, I'm curious to see how those macho types react to being ogled and whistled at."

"They ought to love it." Marta assumed Derek would be in his element.

"They *imagine* they'll love it. In reality, that kind of treatment is demeaning." Bitterness underscored Elise's tone. "I spent my high-school years playing up my appearance. What did it get me? Pursued by guys with sex on their minds and resented by the girls."

As an adult, Elise appeared to have gone overboard in the opposite direction. Marta gathered that, except for tutoring on Saturdays, the officer spent most of her free hours at the gym. She could use both a more positive mind-set and a few girlfriends.

Impulsively, Marta said, "If you aren't busy on Sunday, why don't you join Connie and Rachel and me for dinner." Fearing Elise was about to refuse, she added, "It's my birthday. But don't bring a gift! We're just getting together for fun."

The woman's expression softened. "I'd love to. I don't get out nearly enough. But aren't you having a party?"

The previous year, for Marta's thirtieth birthday, her friends had outdone themselves with an ice-cream potluck and a ragtime-piano player. She didn't expect that sort of effort this year, especially in view of the fact that both had married and become adoptive mothers within the past six months. "It's my thirty-first birthday. Not a milestone like last year."

"In any case, I appreciate the invitation," Elise said. "Where and what time?"

Marta was providing details when a movement by the elevator bank caught her eye. She couldn't deny a tingle of excitement at the sight of Derek's familiar saunter.

Since the wedding, he'd stopped by to say hello a few times but seemed distracted. She'd missed his laughter and joking.

Perhaps dancing together that evening hadn't registered on his radar. For Marta, the experience had fueled her dreams ever since. Despite how often she told herself that it meant nothing, that he'd singled her out because they were both wedding attendants and not for any personal reason, she relished the memory.

She'd dared to fantasize for a few insane hours about bidding for him at the auction. The point was to raise money for the center, after all, and no one would take her interest seriously, least of all Derek. Still, if her true feelings showed on her face, she might permanently damage their easy camaraderie. Besides, who could afford him? Books and tuition, combined with Southern California's notoriously high rents, already strained her budget. Someone was going to win a fabulous night with Sergeant Hit-and-Run, but it wouldn't be her.

Elise indicated a college-age volunteer, who beamed in Derek's direction while ferrying a wheelchair across the lobby. "It's disgusting the way women fall for that alley cat."

"I can't understand it, either." Fortunately, Elise missed the irony in Marta's comment.

Derek didn't appear to notice the admiring volunteer. Instead, he paused to speak to a middle-aged couple waiting on a couch. On a visit to the gift shop earlier to buy a magazine, they'd explained that their son was in surgery.

"I'm heading out on patrol," Elise said. "If I delay too long, the guys might think I'm really injured."

"You *are* really injured!"

"Just bruised. Trauma on the job means a trip to the psychologist." Her friend shuddered. "Don't care to get my head shrunk, thank you." She scooted off.

Derek was still conversing with the couple. Torn between an eagerness to talk to him and a determination to quit breaking her own heart, Marta resumed arranging the costumes.

She studied a pirate hat and eye patch, trying to decide where to put the costume.

"Planning to wear that?" Derek's voice startled her. He must have sneaked up on her.

She recovered fast. "I set it aside for you. Fits your personality, wouldn't you say?"

She held out the hat and patch. After a moment's hesitation, Derek took them.

He slid the elastic around his head until the patch covered his left eye, then adjusted the hat. The rakish effect emphasized the strong lines of his face and the humorous quirk of his mouth.

He studied his reflection in a mirror mounted on the display. "Maybe I should wear it to the auction."

"Your fan club will love it," Marta agreed.

"Don't have one."

"Sure you do," she invented. "Derek's Damsels. Their Web site is full of throbbing hearts and smoochy noises."

"Thanks, but I'll pass." With a smile, he removed the getup. "Not quite my look. Pirates are supposed to be have dark hair. I'm sure it's in the rule book."

"There's a rule book for pirates?"

"Hollywood pirates." He returned the costume pieces.

While stowing them, Marta recalled her earlier curiosity. "Who's that couple in the lobby?"

"Armand Saroyan and his wife. He's my vet." He browsed the display of chocolate bars.

"You have pets?" He'd never mentioned one.

"No." Derek examined a caramel bar. "I occasionally pick up strays in need of assistance."

Marta didn't associate such a task with the community relations office. "Isn't that Animal Control's responsibility?"

"I do it on my own time." Choosing two bars, he paid with a five-dollar bill. "I'm not entirely superficial, you know."

Marta went behind the register to make change. "I never thought you were!"

"Most people do." Wryly, he added, "I guess I encourage them."

"You do project that image." But through the suave veneer, Marta occasionally glimpsed a deeper, troubled soul, which was partly what drew her to him. "Underneath, you're complex."

"Sounds as if you've performed an analysis." He leaned against the counter. "Why so curious?"

Risky territory. "I'm interested in what makes people tick," Marta generalized. "And I get the sense that something's worrying you."

He remained silent. To give him space, she opened a small box of puzzles that had arrived that morning and busied herself affixing price tags.

"Okay, here's the problem," Derek announced at last. "Joel's planning to flaunt his stuff tomorrow night. Not exactly a stripper act, but close. He's inspired the other guys into competing for the highest bid."

"Beefcake isn't your style." Derek didn't have to work at being sexy, although Marta would duct-tape her mouth shut before she'd say so.

"Exactly. So—" He halted.

Marta quit fussing with the merchandise. "Derek."

"Yes?"

"Finish your sentence."

"Which sentence?" His forehead furrowed.

"The one in which you ask my advice," she explained. "I gather your pride demands that you win this little contest."

"Sure, I'd like to," he responded with an edge of irritation. "I don't see what that has to do with pride."

"Talk nice to me or I'll throw you out on your ear," she threatened.

A killer dent appeared in one cheek. "You're a powerhouse when you let rip, Marta. You ought to show that side of yourself more often."

She'd actually impressed him. Was *that* the key to winning a man's heart—talking tough? The tactic had worked for Connie, who'd bossed Hale for years into fixing her plumbing and hauling groceries. Of course, he'd gladly complied because he was secretly in love with her, an advantage she didn't have with Derek.

Well, if he preferred assertiveness, she'd provide it. "Okay, I'm showing it now. If you'd like me to groom you for tomorrow night, say so."

Derek regarded her approvingly. "I hadn't figured out that that's what I wanted, but you're on target. I need advice on how to knock a roomful of women off their chairs without sacrificing my dignity."

If a female friend had sought her counsel, Marta knew

how she'd reply. She resolved to treat Derek the same way. "You have to choose the right image. I'd better drop by your place and sort through your closet."

"Okay," he replied. "What time are you free?"

He'd agreed! Marta could hardly believe it. "I get off at six."

"Let's say my place around seven." He scribbled the address on the back of a business card. Marta recognized the location as a condo development on the west side of town.

"I'll be there." She kept her tone casual. No big deal. Just a couple of friends hanging.

"Until then. And thanks." With an easy wave, Derek ambled off.

Marta felt like a teenager who'd received a rock star's autograph. Better yet, an invitation to the star's private quarters.

This isn't a date, you idiot. He asked you to help him bowl over women so he can score more points than his buddies. And to raise money for the center, she noted more charitably.

Well, she was up for that. Marta, the newly assertive best friend to Villazon's killer hunk.

Not the role she would have chosen, but a definite step forward.

THE ALARM ON Derek's watch buzzed soon after he arrived home that evening. Perversely, he hated the computerized device with its multiple alarm settings, although his friends considered it cool. To him, it served as an electronic jailer and a reminder of circumstances he'd rather forget.

The doctor had changed his dosage twice, seeking optimal results and as few side effects as possible. Currently, Derek had to swallow a pill three times a day. Mercifully, the initial nausea had passed and his symptoms hadn't worsened.

They hadn't entirely disappeared, either. Stiffness in his legs. A recurrent tremor in his hand. Fortunately, there'd been no repetition of an episode last year when, under stress due to a heavy load of investigations, Derek had endured severe shaking for several agonizing seconds. He'd been alone in his car—parked, thank heaven—and had recovered quickly. But after months spent ignoring small problems, that incident had forced him to seek medical attention.

A pinched nerve or deep muscle strain, he'd assumed. He'd gone for a checkup, expecting to be told he needed a week's vacation or, at worst, surgery.

A raft of tests had failed to yield definitive results, so the general practitioner sent him to a neurologist. After a brief examination, the man had delivered the news. He'd spoken calmly and sympathetically, assuring Derek that he could lead a relatively normal life and that research offered hope.

Despite the kindness, the man might as well have smacked Derek with a baseball bat. The diagnosis had roared into his brain like a 747 landing with reverse thrusters, obliterating all other thoughts.

Parkinson's disease.

Origin unknown. Might be genetic, or the result of exposure to environmental toxins, or something else as yet unidentified, the neurologist had said. In any case, the disease involved the deterioration of nerve cells that produced an essential brain chemical called dopamine. The short version: the loss had begun to affect Derek's ability to control physical movement. Sooner or later, he was going to deteriorate.

A life sentence with no cure. He'd never again be simply Derek Reed, a guy who skied and played soccer and, at a last-minute suggestion from a friend, felt free to throw a change of underwear into a pack and go camping.

He'd always have to be careful. Swallow the meds on schedule. Monitor his activities to prevent exhaustion or strain. Otherwise, the doctor had warned, the shaking or other acute symptoms might disable him for a long spell.

In his teens, Derek had felt invulnerable. Later, after he became a police officer, the risks of his profession hadn't daunted him. To remain fit and strong, he'd exercised with weights. He'd known he might fall during a confrontation with a criminal, but he'd never expected treason from within. The discovery filled him with rage.

He'd kept his condition secret from all but the department's top management and meant to go on doing so. He refused to invite one iota of sympathy or, heaven forbid, pity.

As for his personal life, the diagnosis had initially sent Derek on a quest to live full out. His tendency to enjoy the moment while avoiding entanglements had emerged as a mission to confirm that he was still here and still in charge of his fate.

That phase had ended abruptly after an embarrassing episode in which he'd failed to perform sexually, either as a result of the illness or as a side effect of the medication. Since then, Derek had avoided intimacy. He wasn't abandoning sex; he just hadn't figured out what to do about it yet.

This bachelor auction didn't bother him because he intended to leave the winning lady untouched, except perhaps for a good-night kiss. Neither he nor any of the other guys was for sale in *that* sense.

What did bother him, as he'd told Marta, was the prospect of occupying center stage during the bidding. He nursed a deeper fear than merely drawing a low bid; it was fear of stumbling, or trembling, or otherwise revealing his symptoms in a context where he couldn't disguise them. To be unmasked in front of the world was the stuff of nightmares, even for a seasoned cop.

The pill went down like a lump of coal. Derek waited long enough to let his empty stomach absorb it, then microwaved a frozen dinner. Afterward, he toured the lower floor of his condo in a search of compromising material, tucking away an article on Parkinson's research that he'd printed from the Internet.

He wished now that he hadn't bought a two-story unit, but five years ago he'd fallen in love with the view of surrounding hills. So far, the stairs didn't pose a serious obstacle, though, and he supposed he could install a chairlift if his condition got worse.

When it got worse. Maybe not for fifteen or twenty years, the doctor had said. But barring a medical breakthrough, the disease would run its inexorable course.

Derek returned his focus to the surroundings. A bit stark for Marta's taste, he suspected, but perfect for his. The decorator had furnished the place in neutral colors and utilitarian materials, as requested. Hardwood floors, clean lines—easy to maintain and uncluttered.

Funny thing about women. Five minutes after he got involved with one, she tried to personalize the place, scattering fashion magazines, buying candles, that sort of thing. Why couldn't they understand that he *liked* empty space?

Since he had a few minutes to spare, Derek flipped through an agenda for the next city council meeting, searching for items that concerned the police. He and the chief always attended the sessions as a precaution, anyway, since even if nothing appeared on the agenda, you never could tell what issue an audience member might raise.

At the same time, he tuned in to the flow of traffic outside, listening for the rumble of a car pulling into the condo lot. Marta had arrived at the rehearsal dinner in an aging and rather noisy compact on which she claimed to have replaced all the major parts. "That makes it practically new," she'd kidded.

Into Derek's thoughts flashed an image of her stepmother strutting through the reception wearing thousands of dollars in jewelry. Hard to picture a father behaving so callously toward his only child, yet Marta had defended him.

Despite what she'd endured, she maintained an upbeat attitude. Visiting with her provided Derek with welcome relief from his dark moods.

The sound of the doorbell startled him. How had he missed the thrum of her car?

Marta waited on the porch, holding a large red shopping bag that bore the name Connie's Curios. The porch light brought out the brightness in her face.

"Hi!" She sounded breathless. "Lemme in. My arm's falling off."

Derek moved aside. In a deep-pink blouse and jeans that emphasized her shapely curves, she softened the sharp edges of the decor merely by entering.

"What've you got there?" He relieved her of the bag and peered inside. The crown of a hat peeked through tissue paper.

"Props." Marta dropped her purse to the floor. "I wasn't sure what we'd find in your wardrobe, so I borrowed a selection from Connie's shop. She has more stock than I do."

"I'll reimburse any cost," he promised.

"You only need to pay for what you keep. The rest goes back." She indicated the kitchen, divided from the main room by an eat-in peninsula. "Okay if I pour myself a glass of water? I walked from her shop rather than drove. It's only a couple of blocks and I figured the condo development might be chintzy about guest parking."

That explained why he hadn't heard her arrival. "Go right ahead."

He should have offered her a drink, Derek realized, but she'd already breezed past him, boosted herself against the rim of the counter and fetched a glass from overhead. He hadn't noticed before how high the cabinets were.

"There's bottled water in the fridge." Belatedly, he started in her wake. "Let me fix that for you."

She filled her glass from the tap. "I'm not fussy." She took a deep gulp.

"Your rehab paid off," he told her. "The walk here doesn't seem to have fazed you."

She set the glass in the sink. "I had to be in shape to return to school. Have you visited the Cal State Fullerton campus lately? It's huge."

"I graduated from Long Beach." That was another of several California State University campuses in the greater Los Angeles area. "You've got how many semesters left?"

"Technically only three, but since I can't carry a full load, it'll take years," she admitted. "Then a year of education classes, plus student teaching. By the time I earn my credentials, I'll be ancient. Say, about your age."

He chuckled, accustomed to the friendly jibes. A few weeks ago, when a woman had tried to pick him up in full view of the hospital gift shop, Marta had waited until the lady left and then cracked, "I'll bet you remind the poor dear of her beloved grandfather."

She didn't spare herself, either. He hadn't forgotten how, after congratulating him on his promotion to sergeant a couple of years ago, she'd indicated her scars and remarked, "I earned my stripes, too."

"Must be hard to put in the hours studying," he said. "You have a busy schedule." Work, volunteering and, although she'd never mentioned a boyfriend, a woman as effervescent as Marta must snare plenty of dates, too.

"Not hard at all, because I love it. I can hardly wait to get in front of a classroom. I'd give up sleeping if that would help me graduate sooner."

Or you could shame that father of yours into spending half the money on you that he wastes on his wife's finery. Then you could study full-time. Derek withheld the comment. He was the last person to lecture anyone about dealing with family, considering his prickly relationship with *his* parents.

Before he registered her intention, Marta grabbed the shopping bag and started up the stairs. "Let's poke into that closet and see what we can do," she announced as she climbed.

When he straightened the condo, Derek had forgotten she'd planned to dig through his clothes. He strained to recall if he'd left any incriminating information in sight upstairs.

Probably. He did a lot of reading related to his condition. Yet, short of yanking Marta off the stairs, he had no way to stop her. In fact, she'd already reached the second-floor landing.

All he could do was follow.

Chapter Three

Marta's friends accused her—admiringly—of having a lot of nerve. She'd possessed the brass to cofound a homework center even though she hadn't finished college, and she'd taken the initiative to stock the gift shop with new merchandise based on her personal taste. Overall, she'd racked up enough successes to impress Connie.

Barreling up to a man's bedroom, especially *Derek's* bedroom, without waiting for permission took even more guts, but inhaling his masculine scent had filled her with yearning from the moment she entered the condo. Either she treated him with her usual lighthearted bluster or he might start to intimidate her.

Should she reveal so much as a hint of her feelings, Marta would never dare to face him again. In the short run, acting pushy took less fortitude.

Which is why she arrived alone at the top of the stairs. From the landing, she peered out a window that overlooked the center of the complex, which had beautiful landscaping, a pool and a clubhouse. Marta doubted she'd ever be able to afford anything this plush, but homeownership in pricey Southern California wasn't what mattered most. A person had to keep her priorities straight. Otherwise she might abandon the difficult path leading to the career she desired.

Behind her, Derek strolled up the stairs in leisurely fashion. Since he seemed relaxed about her intrusion, Marta kept going. Thank goodness for the chance to collect her wits and recover from the impact of seeing the man in a black T-shirt and snug-fitting chinos.

Traversing the hallway, she glanced into two bedrooms, one containing a desk and file cabinet, the other appointed with exercise equipment. Buying such a large place might have been simply a wise financial investment—or it might signal a nesting instinct.

Derek with a baby in his arms. Giving horsey rides to a toddler. Dancing an anniversary waltz with his wife. She'd be tall and slender, an elegant woman like he usually dated.

I'll be fine with it. I've got my own plans.

As for children, one of Marta's greatest fears after awakening in the hospital had been that her injuries might preclude childbearing. Mercifully, they did not. Although she doubted she'd ever meet another man as exciting as Derek, she didn't need to marry a fantasy. Someone dependable, kind and loving would suit her fine.

At the end of the hall, she found the master bedroom furnished with the same simplicity as the living room: a hardwood floor, a king-size bed and a Scandinavian-style bureau. No trace of feminine slippers or lingerie lying about. Did that indicate he wasn't involved with anyone, or simply that he was tidy?

Embarrassed by the direction of her thoughts, Marta glanced at the sprinkling of magazines atop an end table. Medical journals, she noted with interest. She'd read a lot of those during her rehab. She flipped open the top journal and scanned the table of contents. Avian influenza...Parkinson's disease...new approaches to trauma. Presumably, that related to the abuse-prevention program. Good for Derek, searching for ways to help others.

Marta swiveled as he entered the room. He studied her with an unreadable expression. "Find anything worth reading?"

She set down the magazine. "That stuff about trauma. I'm impressed that you're doing research for your job."

"I don't deserve any special credit," he responded quietly. "Did you inspect the closet?"

"Not yet." In fact, she didn't see one. "Where is it?"

He jerked his chin toward the bathroom. A confined space, and even more personal than the bedroom. Rejecting a twinge of cowardice, Marta led the way.

Oversize tub plus separate shower, a skylight and a large, etched-glass window—palatial appointments, maintained with austere neatness. No feminine things on the counter, she registered.

Marta set down her sack. "This is a bathroom any woman would kill for. Nice going, Sarge."

"I enjoy my comforts." He grinned lazily. "Care for a dip? That's a whirlpool bath. Very soothing."

"Forgot my swimsuit," she retorted.

"No problem." He appeared to be enjoying the implication.

Which was that he wouldn't mind seeing Marta naked in his bathtub. Even as her pulse speeded, she registered that flirting had become second nature to Derek, regardless of whether he nurtured any interest in the woman. Besides, the last thing she'd do in front of this gorgeous man was strip off her clothes and display the scars zigzagging across her midsection.

"I charge for a peek at my maze," Marta said. "Several carnivals have offered large sums."

His teasing expression vanished. "Didn't occur to me that might be a sensitive subject. Sorry."

"Let me ask your opinion," she retorted. "I've been considering incorporating them into one large tattoo. Which would be sexier—a map of Las Vegas or a picture of a goddess throwing lightning bolts?"

Derek studied her with unaccustomed gentleness. "You don't have to act flip. I would never make fun of you."

Unexpectedly, the compassion in his voice nearly brought

tears. Averting her face, Marta blinked them away. "I'm perfectly capable of making fun of myself."

"So I've observed." Drawing nearer, he touched her arm. "Do guys give you a hard time about your injuries?"

No, because I never let anyone close enough. She met his gaze. "Not since I decked the first one who tried. He'll be out of traction any year now."

Derek's deep amber eyes loomed disturbingly near. "You've developed self-protection to an art form. But you don't need it with me."

Warmth radiated from where his hand rested on her sleeve. Crazily, Marta imagined he might be about to kiss her. She'd dreamed of this moment for so long it had become almost palpable.

But one kiss would threaten a friendship she valued beyond measure. As for his comment about not requiring defenses, the one person she *most* had to guard against was Derek.

Pulling away, Marta snatched several hats from the bag and set them on the counter. Beside them, she placed a leather belt with a silver buckle. "Okay, big guy, choose your props."

He focused on the array of accessories. "What is all this?"

"I figured the best tactic would be to represent a classy character." Marta gave him a deerstalker hat. "Let's start with Sherlock."

A bit reluctantly, Derek clapped on the checked hat with front-and-rear brims, and fixed his attention on the mirror. "Interesting, but…"

"If you've got a tweed coat, it might work." She feigned her usual good cheer, while her heart rate hurtled along.

He adjusted the brims at various angles, without improving the impression. "Nice idea, but it isn't me."

Marta had to admit he lacked the thin, angular build of the actors she'd seen portray Sherlock Holmes. "I guess not. Scratch that one."

He swapped the deerstalker for the Stetson. "You think I could pass as a cowboy?"

Her finger traced the tooled surface of the belt. "Worth a try."

"Yes, ma'am." He cocked the hat atop his blond hair. To her eye, he resembled a country-music singer, sexy enough to drive any roomful of females to loosen their purse strings. And probably their clothing, too.

He slid the belt through his jeans loops. At this point, Joel would probably have executed a slow pelvic grind for good measure, but that wasn't Derek's style. Instead, a charming devil of a cowpoke peered into the mirror for a second and then faded, leaving a rather uncomfortable man in his stead. "Sorry, no."

"You know what your problem is?" Marta demanded.

"Too boring and conventional?" He regarded her challengingly.

"Too much dignity." She reclaimed the hat and stuffed the crown with tissues before stowing it in the sack. After he removed the belt, Marta wound it into a circle, aware of the body warmth clinging to the leather.

"Any more ideas?"

"There's baseball." She produced a blue cap bearing the words *Con Amore*, the name of Connie's new line of designer accessories, and a blue-and-white-striped polo shirt with the same name woven above the breast pocket. "What do you think?"

Derek shook his head. "I'm not the baseball type. Used to enjoy soccer, but I've outgrown it." Politely, he amended, "I appreciate your efforts and, given the short notice, you've produced some creative options. I suppose I'll just have to walk out and stand there like a block."

Disappointed to have let him down, Marta tucked the items out of sight. "Is there anything you *are* willing to do? Push-ups, for instance?"

He stared into space for so long that she began to fear

she'd offended him. Abruptly, his fingers began tapping his thigh, a movement that seemed almost involuntary. She'd never seen Derek act this fidgety before.

"Are you okay?" Perhaps he had a migraine.

He blinked away the hesitation. "No push-ups. I can't move around the stage."

"Why not?" He'd moved well enough on the dance floor.

Derek folded his arms defensively. "As I mentioned, I used to play soccer, and my old injuries have caught up with me. Once in a while I run into a balance problem. If I stumble or trip, the guys would rag on me forever."

He evidently found the confession painful. The fact that he'd divulged this much to Marta said a lot about their friendship.

Entering his mid-thirties and being forced to deal with approaching middle age must hit such an active guy hard. By contrast, Marta had long ago abandoned her own notions of youthful perfection.

"I'm the right person to ask about clumsiness," she said. "Don't forget, I had to relearn how to walk." Noting his rigid stance, she stood on tiptoe and reached up to massage his shoulders. "Relax."

Beneath her probing fingers, some of the tightness eased. "You missed your calling. Should have been a masseuse."

"I'm not that talented." Besides, because of their height difference, she had to balance against him. The sensation of his hard back muscles beneath her breasts lit up Marta's nerve endings.

"I beg to differ," Derek murmured.

"Also, my hands aren't strong enough." She finished kneading and stepped aside. "If I were a real masseuse, I'd make you lie down." Hearing the possible double meaning, she amended, "On a table."

He smiled. "You're cute when you blush."

"All the guys tell me that." Her cheeks heated even more.

"Does your boyfriend? Or do you have a boyfriend?" He remained angled toward her, disturbingly close.

"Not at the moment." A very long moment. The ten-year variety, Marta mused, since that was how long she'd gone without a guy. "Returning to our subject…"

"Massages, as I recall," he drawled.

"The auction!"

"Ah, yes." He conceded the point with apparent reluctance. "Pray continue."

She gathered her concentration. "How about a presentation that allows you to simply strike a pose?"

"The less I move around the better," Derek agreed.

Marta recalled how handsome he'd looked at the wedding. "Do you own a tuxedo?"

"If you'd rifled through my closet as you threatened, you'd know the answer," he commented.

"You could just tell me."

"And spoil the fun? Besides, you might devise an even better idea while you're in there."

She doubted she'd find a better idea than a tux, but curiosity won. "Okay, you asked for it." She opened the door to the walk-in closet.

Venturing into the ripple of pheromones emanating from crisp jeans, slacks, tees and business shirts felt like being wrapped in Derek's arms. A change in air pressure marked the moment when he slipped in behind her. His presence jolted Marta almost as if they were physically connected.

"To your left." His baritone restored her to reality.

Staring at the spot he indicated, she identified the pieces of the penguin suit arrayed on hangers. "So you *do* own the tux."

"Bought it when I was in high school. I can't tell you how much I've saved on rentals."

She visualized the impact he would make on the small stage at the homework center. "Just stroll out with that James Bond sophistication of yours and you'll be the hit of the evening."

"I won't come across as dull?"

Marta almost laughed. "Not a chance," she said. "Let the

other guys show off. The contrast will emphasize how polished you are."

He nodded in approval. "I love the idea. Can you arrange for me to go last? That'll make more impact."

"I'm sure Yolanda will agree." Marta ducked beneath his arm and escaped the confines. Too personal and intimate. Derek might be immune, but she was not, by a long shot.

He sauntered out, clearly pleased with the decision. "This is perfect. Thanks, Marta."

"My pleasure." She collected the bag. "I'll be there to cheer you on."

"No fair bidding on another guy and breaking my heart," he joked.

She sought an equally lighthearted rejoinder. "Don't worry. I won't go blowing my tuition money on some guy." She eased out of the bathroom, chattering because it was more comfortable than dealing with silence. "Don't forget to arrive early. I'd recommend wearing your costume from home. The only dressing facility is the men's room."

"I'm sure I'll manage," he commented dryly.

"Best to park across the street at the high school. Leave our lot for patrons." Villa Corazon occupied the city's former community center, a Spanish-style building that had originally been a church. "I've got to head over there now to help with the decorating."

"What kind of decorating?" A dubious note crept into his voice. "No boudoir themes, I hope."

"Certainly not." Marta spoke over her shoulder as they went down the hall. "Connie's borrowing spotlights from the high school, and she talked a video store into lending us posters. Glamorous, not amorous. Yolanda was firm about that."

"Glamorous, huh? I hope we don't disappoint." Quickly, he amended, "Those other guys, anyway."

"Villazon's bachelors are the best!"

"I'll second that."

As they started down the stairs, one knee must have given him trouble, because he was limping. He'd mentioned balance problems, not stiff muscles. He really should reduce his workouts, Marta thought.

On the ground floor, she hurried toward the exit. No sense risking further proximity. She only hoped her reactions to him hadn't been too obvious. "See you tomorrow tonight."

"I owe you big-time for rescuing me," Derek called.

"You cops are the ones who rescue people," she responded. A flash of chagrin on his face was the last thing she saw before closing the door.

As Marta descended to the sidewalk, the truth dawned. She'd heard speculation about the reasons behind Derek's assignment to his new post and had noted his less-than-enthusiastic comments. Now she put two and two together.

The physical restrictions he'd mentioned must have forced him to leave active policing. Although his current work included crime prevention, he evidently felt like an exile, and she'd just rubbed salt into his wounds.

At least he'd trusted her enough to share his concerns. Henceforth, Marta resolved to resume her role as cheerleader and confidante, with more understanding than before. As for the vibes flowing between them, those simply reflected his natural sensuality. How fortunate that she hadn't complicated the situation by yielding to the urge to kiss him.

DEREK DROPPED onto a stool at the dining peninsula and attempted to sort through his emotions. Primarily relief that he'd managed to convey the gist of his symptoms without revealing his diagnosis.

He felt something else, too—an unfamiliar warmth for Marta. He'd become aware of her in a new way physically while they were examining the costumes. But he couldn't allow anything to come of that.

Restlessly, he wandered into the kitchen and poured a drink

of water. His medication tended to dehydrate him, so he downed the contents in a few gulps and set the glass beside Marta's.

Derek wished he understood why he quickly grew impatient with relationships. Perhaps if he had a tragic tale of lost love, that might explain it, but although a few of his affairs had lasted for a year or longer, none had truly touched his heart.

Must be a quirk of his personality. Growing up, he hadn't fit into his family, always feeling like an outsider, especially compared to his younger brother and sister. Were it not for the photos taken of him with his mother at the hospital and the resemblance between him and his father, he might have believed he was adopted.

Mom and Dad were lawyers, a course his brother had followed and his sister had considered before becoming an accountant. All held advanced degrees, as well as political views far to the left of Derek's.

His parents and younger siblings also shared the same interests: chess, museums, serious films. He'd been the odd kid, stubborn and, as an adolescent, defiant. A loner, impatient with academic subjects, failing to fit in anywhere until he joined the police force.

Now he didn't truly fit in there, either. Despite the doctor's assurances that he might be able to continue working for a decade or longer, his illness had already consigned him to the perimeter. Not only because of his front-office post but because he had to keep the others at bay in order to hide his condition.

If anyone would understand, it might be Marta, given the injuries she'd overcome. But she was too tightly linked to the rest of his circle: friends with Rachel, cousin to Connie, related by marriage to Hale. How unfair to burden her with a secret and expect her to keep it from those dearest to her.

And how uncomfortable to realize that, once she knew the truth, she wouldn't be able to help seeing him differently. Not as a person who, like her, might ultimately regain his health, but as a man destined to deteriorate.

Derek hated this illness and hated his body for betraying him. All the same, tomorrow night he was going to show Joel and the others he was still the sexiest man in Villazon. In later years, when his friends reminisced about the good old days, he hoped they'd remember Derek Reed's triumph at the bachelor auction.

Not much compared to saving lives and bringing down the bad guys, but a victory nonetheless. His spirits rising, Derek won-dered what sort of woman he'd be spending Saturday evening with....

Chapter Four

On Friday after work, Marta arrived at the Villa Corazon center an hour and a half before the scheduled start of the auction. Her back and hips, always vulnerable, ached from her exertions last night helping decorate. As usual, she'd let enthusiasm override her better judgment.

After parking at the high school, Marta limped across the residential street to the stucco building. A banner over the arched front door read Bachelor Auction Tonight 8:00 p.m.! To one side, a placard explained about the center's tutoring program.

This week's edition of the *Voice* had carried a front-page article about the event. Perhaps as a result, more than half the available tickets had sold in advance.

Marta hoped no one planned to jeer or catcall. Most guys might laugh off such behavior, but it would offend Derek. Still, with so many police officers involved, she didn't expect any serious rowdiness.

In the lobby, oversize posters of male movie stars spiced up the usually sedate decor. From the unseen interior echoed a few male and female voices, punctuated by childish shrieks and giggles.

Surprised that Yolanda would allow youngsters to attend, Marta walked to the interior doorway. Skip ran up the aisle in pursuit of Rachel's stepdaughter, Lauren, and had nearly

caught her when Russ swooped in to capture his little girl.
Giving the five-year-old a hug, he informed the kids that they
were going for a walk.

"I'm babysitting tonight," he told Marta as he shepherded
the children past her. "We figured that in case people bring
kids, someone should supervise activities in the playroom,
and I'm nominated." Stocked with toys and books, the room
was used for tutoring five- and six-year-olds, who often had
trouble sitting still.

"Nice of you to pitch in." She ruffled Skip's hair as he went
by.

"Have fun," Russ responded.

Marta descended the aisle and approached Yolanda. The
director stood near the front, supervising nineteen-year-old
Ben Lyons as he adjusted the sound system. Skinny and
freckled, he scrambled to do a good job for his mentor and
landlady. After a fire gutted his apartment the previous spring,
she'd repaired it and rerented to him. Yolanda had disregarded
initial suspicions that Ben, who'd battled a drug problem, might
have triggered the fire with the carelessly discarded marijuana
joint found in his unit.

The blaze had been yet another in a series of embarrassing incidents affecting the police department, now headed by
Ben's father, Chief Will Lyons. Suspicion later fell on Norm
Kinsey, a police lieutenant once fired for prisoner abuse. He'd
returned to town seeking revenge against his former colleagues but had died of a heart attack before he could be
charged with anything, including a possible attempt to frame
the chief's son.

Marta liked Ben and found him eager to please—everyone
except Chief Lyons. Father and son always seemed to rub each
other the wrong way.

"Where are the tickets and my cash box?" she asked.

"Heading our way." Yolanda indicated Rachel, who'd just
emerged from the office wing with an armload of stuff.

"Perfect timing." With Yolanda in charge, Marta had known the event would be smoothly organized. "Good luck tonight."

"We won't need it. Our bachelors are fabulous." The older woman winked. "I'm tempted to try for one myself."

"Go for it!" Too bad they hadn't been able to persuade any older men to volunteer, Marta thought as she joined Rachel. Yolanda, a widow with two grown sons, deserved a second chance at love.

"You'll be a great ticket seller," Rachel said on their way to the foyer. "You'll put everyone in a generous mood."

"Thanks. What's your job tonight?" Marta asked.

"Directing traffic. We're reserving the lot for the elderly and handicapped, and steering the rest of the cars across the road." Rachel's blue blazer and slacks didn't exactly constitute a uniform but, coupled with a large flashlight, gave her an official air.

"Isn't Elise supposed to help?" Marta recalled her mentioning that.

"She got stuck at the jail doing paperwork for a perp. Hope she gets free soon."

Rachel didn't sound concerned. She wasn't easily fazed and never had been. Nearly a dozen years ago, waiting to cross the street to attend police-science classes at college, she'd witnessed a car speeding through a red light and smashing into the passenger side of Connie's sedan. She'd waded in to rescue Marta and, in the long months that followed, had joined Connie as Marta's support system.

Now Rachel strode jauntily out into the October evening. Sitting alone at a card table, Marta double-checked the change in the cash box to ensure that it tallied with the amount Yolanda had written on a sheet. Then she settled into her seat.

Her thoughts immediately flew to Derek. Last night, his concern about her scars had revealed yet another layer to his character. Beneath that tantalizing surface lay a truly kind soul.

Yesterday had also marked the first time Marta experienced the man and his sex appeal at such close range. Easy to understand how women succumbed.

Gratefully, she broke off that train of thought as a radiant Connie breezed in to say hello. She'd been walking on air since her honeymoon in Lake Tahoe.

"Hale's fussing with his microphone," she announced fondly. "I'm glad he doesn't act as emcee for a living!"

"If he did, he'd be used to it," Marta pointed out. "Are the other guys here?" She kept her tone casual.

"A couple of them. Derek hasn't showed yet, but it's early, and he's on last." Despite Marta's efforts at discretion, Connie had long ago learned of her crush. Fortunately, she was too tactful to kid her about it. "Someone should arrive any minute to take tickets at the inner door."

"They won't get past me, and besides, I doubt any of our guests will sneak in." Marta would appreciate the company all the same.

"Elise is still joining us for dinner Sunday, isn't she?" Connie continued.

"I hope so."

"I'm glad you invited her. I've been wanting to get better acquainted." When her phone rang, Connie peered at the display. "It's Hale. He probably messed up his tie or something. Catch you later!" In she went.

Marta tried to squash a tiny selfish streak that wished her friends were raising their usual fuss about her birthday. Such celebrations, for each of them, had assumed added importance after Marta's brush with death. But that was ages ago, and newlyweds had more important matters on their minds.

Zandy Watts, Connie's partner in the new Con Amore line of clothes and accessories, arrived to collect tickets. Short, dark hair laced with gray complemented the fortyish woman's strong features.

"Plan to bid on a fella?" she asked Marta after they exchanged greetings.

"I'm saving my money for tuition," she responded. "How about you?"

"Merely planning to enjoy the show, however much I get to see" came the cheerful response.

Audience members began trickling in. Small groups of women sauntered through the lobby, laughing and egging each other on. Couples entered as well, paying admission for the entertainment value, Marta supposed.

She greeted many of them by name. Thanks to her job at the hospital and her volunteer activities, she had a wide circle of acquaintances.

The bachelors must be entering through the alley door, as instructed, since she didn't see any of them. There'd been a dozen at last count, ranging from emergency-services personnel to a teacher and an attorney.

Marta felt nervous for Derek. Despite his assertive attitude and reputation as a charmer, he was a very private person. He probably wouldn't have volunteered if not for his job.

A flash of auburn hair distracted Marta from her musings. Andrea O'Reilly, a fire investigator, was fishing in her purse for her wallet. "Rachel's got her hands full with the traffic out there," she commented. "Isn't anyone assisting her?"

"Elise got held up at the station," Marta explained.

"I'd pitch in, but I'm determined to land a date with Derek." She forked over a bill.

A sharp pang rose unbidden. "You must like him a lot."

"Just interested in the bragging rights." Cheerfully, Andie collected her change and whisked toward the interior.

Marta knew that with a knockout like Andie, a date that began as a lark might easily develop into more. She didn't want to care, but she did.

Tracy Johnson popped in. At five one, exactly Marta's own height, she looked tiny compared to most of the other women. Her pointy chin and sharp nose gave her an elfin quality, offset tonight by the loose shoulder-length hair she usually wore in a ponytail.

"Don't tell me you plan to bid!" Marta said.

Tracy ducked her head. "The publisher's been pushing me to run more human-interest stuff. I figured I'd spend a couple of hours with the most macho hunk I could find and write a story about it."

Marta's stomach knotted. "Anyone in particular?"

"I considered Sergeant Reed, but that might be awkward, since I'm always contacting him for information," the reporter said. "Any suggestions?"

What a relief. The last thing Derek needed was a smart-aleck write-up in the paper.

Marta blurted the first name that entered her mind. "How about Joel Simmons?"

"Connie's ex?" The newspaper office lay in the same shopping strip as Connie's flagship store, so the women were well acquainted. "Sexy but macho, so I hear. Just the type I'm interested in. The type that deserves a comeuppance."

"Maybe he'll sweep you off your feet," Marta countered.

"Like that's gonna happen!" Chuckling, Tracy moved on.

Marta stayed busy selling admissions for a while. Only a dozen or so tickets remained by the time Chief Lyons arrived accompanied by Captain Ferguson, who'd served as interim chief before Lyons was hired. With the chief a widower and Frank divorced, they'd apparently fallen into the habit of attending public functions together.

"Keeping an eye on the troops?" Marta joked.

A broad-chested fellow with a thin mustache, the chief took her remark seriously. "Showing my approval of a good cause. Hope I don't make the guys self-conscious."

His beefy companion gave Marta a nod. "You shouldn't be stuck out here working. You do get to watch the fun, don't you?"

"Maybe a little," she replied. "But I'm also cashier for the bids."

"Hardworking lady. Good for you." He followed his boss inside.

Zandy wandered over. "Not bad-looking."

"Captain Ferguson?" Marta had never considered the fiftyish man in that light.

"No, the chief. Not exactly approachable, though."

That was an understatement. The man defined "reserved." "I can't imagine going on a date with him!"

"Still grieving over his wife, people say." She'd died five years earlier. "Some folks never recover, I guess." Zandy returned to her post.

Inside, the crowd fell silent. Yolanda's amplified voice drifted out, welcoming the audience and explaining the purpose of the auction. Applause greeted her introduction of master of ceremonies Hale Crandall.

Marta was debating whether she dared step away from the table, when a figure in jeans and a black leather jacket stalked into the foyer from outside. "I can't imagine why Yolanda did that!" Elise Masterson snarled without preamble.

"Did what?" Marta kept her voice low.

Although the officer took the hint, her angry glances toward the front door spoke volumes. "I realize I'm late, but she didn't have to call Vince Borrego to help direct traffic. He shouldn't be within miles of the rest of the police force after the way he dishonored them!"

Yolanda had summoned the town's former, and still controversial, chief to run traffic patrol? As another of the tenants at her fourplex, he occasionally performed odd jobs for her, and Rachel *had* needed assistance. Still, it said a lot about the older woman's faith in the man.

Now a private investigator, he'd attempted to fit into the town since his fall from grace. Although trouble seemed to dog his footsteps and plenty of people believed he would seize any chance to discomfit the new chief, he'd publicly disavowed Norm Kinsey's attempts at revenge.

Furthermore, Vince's daughter, Teri, who operated the home day-care center that Skip and Lauren attended, was very well liked. Married with two children, she had a warm personality and was close to her father.

Elise, who'd suffered Vince's inappropriate advances on duty, had never believed he'd truly reformed. Finding him in what, as a dedicated volunteer, she considered her territory had understandably stoked her fury.

"Surely it's just for tonight," Marta ventured. "There's no reason for him to be involved at the center any further."

"I'm not so sure. He's been putting on this big show of being a dedicated grandfather. Yolanda's too gullible!"

"At least you get to watch the auction this way," Marta pointed out.

"Sounds like it's starting." Still glowering, Elise marched into the auditorium.

Marta could hear Hale gleefully extolling the merits of Bachelor Number One, Brian Phillips, the attorney coordinating Skip's adoption. "A former football player, our first hunk is such a great guy, he's almost put an end to lawyer jokes single-handedly," Hale boomed. "What am I bid?"

Offers started at the previously announced minimum of twenty dollars and soared from there. Marta cast a precautionary glance outside and, with the coast clear, joined Zandy at the inner entrance.

A blond Viking in his late thirties who dominated the stage, Brian wore a football jersey and below-the-knee knit pants with a racing stripe. Helmet tucked beneath one arm, he feigned reaching for a catch.

"Forty-five!" Marta recognized the bidder as Soraya Bloom, who owned the nail boutique next to Connie's Curios.

"Fifty!" That was Dr. Tanith Williams, a pediatrician from

Russ's office who occasionally stopped into Marta's shop for chewing gum.

"Fifty-five!" called Andie O'Reilly. Apparently she'd decided not to wait for Derek.

"Is that all?" Hale scoffed. "Heck, I'd pay more than that to have Brian spend the evening bouncing drunks from one of my parties."

Amid the laughter, the bids rose. A hundred dollars. A hundred and fifty. They reached two twenty-five, with Andie the winner.

Marta released a breath she hadn't known she was holding. She wouldn't mind so much if a woman in her forties like Soraya or Tanith got hold of Derek. Not that men couldn't fall for older women, but the threat didn't seem as great.

The next bachelor, a young employee from the city clerk's office, bounded onto the stage in a lifeguard outfit. Marta retreated to her table.

Andie slipped out. "Weird, huh? Me and a lawyer," she remarked as she wrote a check. Marta tucked it inside the box and penned a receipt.

"Good choice," Zandy affirmed. "Connie says he's a sweetheart."

Andie didn't bother returning to the auditorium. "I'm going to meet my hunk so we can set a date." The bachelors had been instructed to wait in the reception area of the office wing until their buyers contacted them.

The next candidates went more quickly, and Marta stayed busy accepting payments. Soraya landed a firefighter and Tanith a high-school history teacher.

"It's for a good cause," the physician explained with a touch of awkwardness while she paid. "Besides, most men run for the hills when they find out I'm a doctor. It intimidates them."

"I hope you two hit it off," Marta said.

A shrug answered this comment. "In any case, I could use a night out with an intelligent companion."

More women arrived to tender their payments, and Marta began to fear she'd never get a break. At last she did, though, arriving in time to watch Russ's friend Mike Federov take the stage. A child psychologist who'd helped Skip adapt to his new family, he looked open and appealing in a tweed jacket over jeans.

The women jumped right in. Among them was Rosa Mercato, who ran Connie's third shop, located inside a converted pickle factory that held a farmer's market and boutiques.

The bidding had passed a hundred dollars when a new voice called an offer. Startled, Marta realized Elise had joined the competition.

The tough-as-nails policewoman had her eye on a psychologist? Perhaps that wasn't surprising. Unlike most men Elise encountered, he appeared neither pushy nor threatening.

Other women dropped out in the face of one particularly determined woman whom Marta didn't know. But either Elise really liked the guy or simply refused to admit defeat.

At two hundred eighty-five, the challenger withdrew. Elise nodded with satisfaction at winning.

She didn't move from her seat, though. The rules allowed her to pay after the auction's finish, giving bidders a chance to buy more than one romantic evening. Marta suspected her friend was curious to learn how much her colleagues sold for.

Bill Norton, a patrolman in his late twenties, went for two fifty-five. Robbery-homicide detective Jorge Alvarez, a slightly paunchy thirty-six-year-old, brought in one seventy-five. Young detective Kirk Tenille, who performed pushups onstage, drew two hundred and ninety, well above the two-ten that Rosa paid for traffic sergeant Mark Rohan.

The center had earned nearly two thousand dollars so far, and the auction still had a couple of hot ones in store. Including the man foremost in Marta's mind.

Derek must be listening from the wings to the shouting and

cheering. How did he feel? A massage probably wouldn't go amiss at the moment, Marta reflected wistfully. She could use one herself. Hopping up and down to watch wasn't doing *her* soreness any good.

"Hey!" Zandy signaled as a purchaser departed. "Joel's up."

Marta scurried over. Sure enough, Hale had just welcomed his friend onto the stage.

Joel's husky build and clean-cut features drew hearty applause. The watch commander, in exercise shorts and a T-shirt, performed a series of jumping jacks followed by a cartwheel.

"Used to be a gymnast in high school," Marta noted, and wondered what Connie thought of her ex-husband's display.

She could see only her cousin's back and halo of blond hair. Next to Connie, Rachel whistled and stomped the floor. Obviously, she'd suspended traffic duty until after the occasion.

The numbers for Joel rose rapidly past a hundred dollars, then two hundred. Gradually, women dropped out, leaving a nurse, Nancy Nguyen, and a woman Zandy identified as Kat Ayle. She tended bar at Jose's Tavern, a popular after-hours spot for law-enforcement folks.

Joel teased the crowd, winking at one woman and grinning at another before executing a flip that nearly grazed Hale. The emcee retreated with exaggerated alarm. "He's a live one!"

Kat upped her bid. Nancy hesitated. At the record level of three hundred dollars, the battle appeared to be over.

A new voice broke the calm. "Three-oh-five!"

An excited murmur arose as people recognized Tracy Johnson. Joel stopped cavorting to regard her skeptically.

Maybe I shouldn't have suggested him. Marta didn't envy Joel the prospect of having details of his date splashed across the pages of the *Villazon Voice*.

He'd treated Connie poorly during their marriage, ignoring her to spend weekends with his buddies and attempting to control her with putdowns. Still, Marta harbored no grudges against her ex-cousin-in-law. He'd grown a lot since the divorce and she suspected that a more mature Joel might have decent possibilities for a strong woman.

Tracy, of course, only wanted to exploit the guy. Still, he could take care of himself.

Kat opted out. "I'm not bidding against the newspaper on a bartender's income!" she announced.

No one challenged the assumption that the money came from the *Voice* rather than from Tracy personally. Including the reporter herself, Marta observed.

"That sets a record for tonight, with only one bachelor remaining!" Hale whooped. "Congratulations, Joel. Now let's find out if our final candidate can top that."

Joel's competitive instincts appeared to war with his altruistic desire to raise money for the center. After a brief pause, he added, "Yes, ladies, open your purses for Derek Reed!" and trotted off.

Tension spurred twinges in Marta's muscles as Derek sauntered into view. Perfectly groomed, elegant and all male in his tuxedo. A sigh rippled through the crowd.

The smile playing around the corners of his mouth heightened the impact. To Marta, he represented all things desirable and unattainable.

The tall blond man strolled to the emcee's stand and coolly poured himself a drink from the pitcher of water. He settled onto the edge of a table, one foot on the floor, and surveyed the audience as if taking its measure.

"Wow," Zandy murmured. "There's a guy worth paying for."

Exultantly, Marta shared his triumph as the bids started flying. The bartender. The nurse. Women who'd tried and lost before, and others who'd apparently waited until now.

Some were older, some younger, a few quite beautiful. Almost all better dressed and more sophisticated than Marta. She wished—

Tracy's appearance interrupted her train of thought.

"Here's my check." She passed it to Marta. "Thanks for the tip about Joel. He should make an interesting subject."

At the table, Marta scribbled a receipt. "Don't be too hard on the guy."

"Our readers will love it." Tracy folded the receipt into her purse. "Thanks!"

Marta rejoined Zandy. "The amount's gone over three hundred," the woman explained.

"Really?" Fantastic! That meant Derek would best Joel, as he'd wished.

It also meant the women wanted him badly. Despite the disclaimers about the auction being merely for fun, Marta had noticed that many considered this an opportunity to meet eligible males.

Inside the main room, someone had offered three hundred ten. A pause extended until a familiar voice cried, "Three-fifteen!"

From the stage, Hale frowned at the audience. "Hey! That's my wife!"

Why would Connie bid on Derek? Puzzled, Marta gripped the door frame. It made no sense, unless...

"Don't worry! It's for a friend!" Rachel hollered.

"I'll thank you to refer to our dashing bachelor as 'he' rather than 'it,'" Hale rejoined.

"Okay, *he's* for a friend," Connie responded merrily.

As her cousin returned to the fray, the grim truth struck Marta. Her friends weren't deemphasizing her birthday celebration this year. Instead, they'd planned a surprise treat without considering that, in the process, they were announcing to the world the humiliating fact that Marta Lawson had a crush on Sergeant Hit-and-Run.

Marta wished her friends had forgotten the occasion entirely. Or that she might become invisible for, say, the next couple of years.

Instead, she stood there frozen, awaiting the outcome.

Chapter Five

The smile on Derek's face hardened into a mask. He doubted even the most enthusiastic of the other guys had truly enjoyed the experience once they got up here onstage, and he for one absolutely loathed being treated like cattle.

It's for a good cause for a good cause for a good cause. The words repeated through his mind. Sitting with apparent ease and maintaining an air of savoir-faire took more concentration than one might expect, but he managed to maintain his composure.

Derek scarcely noticed who was bidding, except when Hale mentioned his wife. Then he caught sight of Connie waving.

She was bidding for a friend, Rachel said. So they intended him for Marta's birthday present, did they?

The realization eased his stress. Now, *that* wouldn't be bad. He could relax in Marta's company.

She was peeking in the entrance, her eyes round and her color pale beneath the fluorescent lights. She looked more embarrassed than thrilled. Marta never intentionally thrust herself into the spotlight, probably because she was self-conscious about her limp and scars. Well, any person unable to ignore a few surface imperfections and appreciate the bubbly spirit underneath didn't deserve her friendship.

The bidding went to three thirty-five before Connie nailed

the purchase. She and Rachel high-fived each other when Hale announced their victory.

Derek felt almost guilty taking money for something he'd have done for free if they'd asked. But of course, the funds went to the center. Besides, he'd won the informal contest with Joel.

Once the clapping died, the audience began to disperse. For an uneasy moment as Derek tried to rise, he feared his muscles had locked in place. A slight push against the table hoisted him upright, however.

"Fine job." Hale clapped his shoulder. "You knocked 'em dead."

"Couldn't have done it without you."

The two descended together from the stage and moved into a side hallway. In the office wing was a crush of people. Fellow bachelors, bidders, volunteers, Tracy Johnson writing down quotes and Yolanda thanking everyone. Two women stood with their gazes glued to a firefighter who'd stripped to the waist while changing from a soccer jersey into a sweatshirt.

Derek stepped into the records room to collect his jacket. He emerged to see Will Lyons congratulating the men.

"Great job, guys." The chief shook hands with Joel.

"Thanks. It was fun." Joel made room for Derek.

"You did the force proud, Sergeant," Lyons greeted him.

"The center's a worthwhile cause."

The chief stopped on the verge of replying. Judging by his narrowed eyes, he'd spotted something or someone unpleasant.

Turning, Derek caught sight of Vince Borrego talking to Yolanda in the small, adjacent reception area. Well, that explained it. Didn't their former leader have better sense than to hang around a place crawling with the coworkers he'd dishonored?

The old chief had gotten off easy, in Derek's opinion. True, the man had been forced into retirement and his marriage had crumbled. Nevertheless, Norm Kinsey had lost not only his job but also his pension. His offense—abusing a prisoner—had been so serious that some critics contended he should have received jail time. Still, Borrego had attempted to white-wash Kinsey's misdeed, which, for a man in a position of authority, made him equally culpable in Derek's view.

Their betrayal of the department's ethical standards felt personal. Derek had admired those men when he'd joined the force twelve years ago. He hadn't forgiven Borrego, and neither, to his knowledge, had anyone else at the bureau.

"What a great idea!" Ben Lyons, whose thin figure must have been hidden by Borrego's bulk, shifted into view as he addressed Yolanda.

What was a great idea?

"We should discuss this in private," the center's director told Vince. "Of course I appreciate your interest." She glanced at Will. "Your son performed miracles with our old sound system tonight, Chief."

"Glad he could contribute." That was Will's manner, cool and guarded. Probably not quite the reaction Ben had hoped for, though, judging by a flash of disappointment on his face.

How *did* people repair fences with rebellious kids? Even fifteen years past his adolescence, Derek had never established with his parents the kind of rapport they fell into so easily with his younger siblings.

"Yo, Derek." Connie dodged between a firefighter and one of the bidders. "Tomorrow night at seven, okay? Dinner and dancing. I'll give you Marta's address."

"Maybe we should plan our own date," he countered.

"It's for her birthday," Connie continued fiercely. "She's going to have an absolutely fabulous experience, top-drawer, elegant and memorable. *Comprende?*"

"You mean we can't go down to the county dump and watch the trucks unload?" he asked.

Connie issued an unwilling chuckle. "You better be kidding."

Her husband joined them, his expression mildly perplexed.

"You could have warned me, Con. My bride was bidding for another guy, and in public, yet!"

"Sorry. I didn't think of that," she admitted. "It's for Marta's birthday."

"That's a generous present," Hale said. "Not that I object, but I wouldn't figure Derek for her type."

The man had a point. Why *had* Connie and Rachel singled him out? "Dr. Federov might have been more to her taste," Derek agreed, although he didn't like to think about Marta falling for someone so, well, bland.

A blink of hesitation, and then Connie said, "We went for the sexiest bachelor on the block. Only the best for my cousin! Well, second best, since the emcee wasn't available."

Hale beamed. "Now, *there's* a response I like."

"On that note, we'd better collect our son." Connie patted Derek's arm. "You have our phone number. Call me tomorrow for directions."

"Will do."

Left alone, Derek tried to spot Marta. No sign of her, although the crowd was thinning. Perhaps she'd remained in the auditorium.

He glanced into the large room. Thanks to a swarm of volunteers, tables and desks had already replaced the rows of seats. Atop a ladder, Rachel detached one of the few remaining posters.

Marta must have left. Too bad. Derek would have liked a word with her.

Outside, he retrieved the sedan he'd bought six months earlier to replace his low-slung sports car. Easier to slide in and out of, and it came with a superior sound system.

He turned onto Arches Avenue where, despite the relatively early hour, traffic was light. Villazon wasn't a party town like, say, Huntington Beach.

Ahead, a pickup sped along, weaving in its lane. In no mood to ruin his evening with a traffic stop, Derek nevertheless slowed and kept the vehicle in sight, in case it posed a danger to other motorists.

The guy zipped onto a side street, taking the corner too fast. Because of the spotty lighting, Derek didn't get a clear view of what happened next. A blur near the pavement…a furry shape flying through the air…a sharp yip… The pickup rolled on, its driver oblivious or indifferent.

Although Derek would have loved to bring the jerk to account, checking on the animal's well-being seemed more important. After rounding the corner, he stopped in a safe spot and exited, holding a flashlight. The blanket and medium-size cage he carried in the trunk could wait till he assessed the situation.

On the sidewalk, he approached the crumpled shape with caution. A circle of light revealed a spotted dog of mixed breed, whimpering with pain and fear.

"Are you hurt, pooch?" he asked. Shock might also account for the dog's reaction, although normally an injured animal ran away. Crouching, Derek registered the presence of a collar and tags. Only an irresponsible owner would allow a dog to run free; perhaps this one had escaped. "It's okay, boy. I won't hurt you."

Since the animal neither growled nor flattened its ears, Derek extended his free hand to be sniffed. A pang in his shoulder caused his arm to jerk, which must have frightened the dog. Whining, it lumbered to its feet and loped off, favoring one leg.

Chasing would only scare it into running faster. Besides, Derek didn't put much faith in his sprinting powers.

He followed the animal until it vanished between two houses. Since it was running freely now and probably lived nearby, he retreated to the car.

Out of nowhere, rage filled him, entirely out of proportion to the seriousness of the incident. Maybe that twinge had nothing to do with Parkinson's disease, but Derek had always relied on his physical strength. Now he no longer trusted his own body.

He gripped the steering wheel. He was going to lick this

disease, he reminded himself. Research promised new treatments, even possible cures. Something had to come along, because Derek couldn't imagine a future as an invalid.

He gave the area a last visual sweep. Seeing no sign of the dog, he resumed the drive home.

Maintaining a pose onstage had left him achy all over, although at least he'd pulled off the auction with pizzazz. Dinner and dancing? He hoped Marta wouldn't mind taking things a little easier than that tomorrow.

Regardless of what Connie had in mind, perhaps the two of them could share a casual supper and spend the evening at the movies. Marta would probably prefer that to some romantic nonsense, anyway.

MARTA AWOKE on Saturday determined to call the whole thing off. After the auction, she'd tried in vain to find a moment alone with Connie and Rachel. But too many other people were around, and besides, she hadn't wanted to attract Derek's attention.

Of course, she reflected as she sat on the floor performing a series of stretching exercises, surely she could feign indifference for one evening. Couldn't she?

Ordinarily, yes, except that Derek instinctively moved on a woman, as she'd seen during their encounter at his condo. One kiss and she'd fall into his arms.

Would that be so terrible?

Yes, because once she felt his powerful body against hers, she wouldn't be able to resist giving him anything he wanted. She was already half in love with the guy. To fall the rest of the way would spell disaster.

In a postage-stamp clear space at the center of the studio apartment, Marta launched into a series of sit-ups. Why did she have to fall for the biggest ladies' man in Villazon, anyway?

In high school, she'd had no trouble attracting boyfriends, usually the easygoing sort. During senior year, she'd hit it off with a guy named Joey, whom she'd dated right through homecoming, the prom and graduation.

They'd drifted apart after Joey joined the army and she enrolled at Cal State Fullerton. Letters and e-mails gradually diminished, and when they met at Christmas, they'd experienced only a faint nostalgia.

Caught up in studying for a teaching career, Marta had dated only casually in college. Then the crash, followed by years of surgery and rehab, had torn her life apart.

By the time the doctors declared her healed, Marta had inexplicably developed a craving for a guy completely out of her league. The fact that she liked him as a person made the situation even tougher.

Keeping him at a distance had become essential. Much as she hated disappointing her friends, she had to say no. Since Connie and Rachel both recognized at least some of her feelings for Derek, she supposed she might as well level with them.

A rap at the door startled her. Who could be dropping by at 9:00 a.m.? She hadn't eaten breakfast and was still in her pajamas.

Puzzled, she undid the locks. In sauntered her cousin, effortlessly attractive in designer slacks, silk shell and a short jacket. Beside her was Elise, wearing the usual off-duty jeans and sweatshirt.

Marta wondered if Connie had somehow confused their two policewoman friends. "Where's Rachel?"

"She had to work." Elise cleared her throat. "I heard them discussing a makeover and asked if I could tag along. I'd like to make a good impression on Mike tonight."

"Makeover?" Uh-oh. "I'm fine the way I am."

Connie surveyed the poodle-print pajamas. "Like that?"

"You know what I mean!" Marta hadn't asked for coddling and, worse, she could hardly confess her painful secret in front of Elise. "Besides, I haven't had breakfast."

Connie headed for the kitchen, where she set out Marta's

cereal and removed the nonfat milk from the fridge. "Eat while I tell you the plan."

"What plan?"

"First we hit the Brea Mall and buy you a new outfit. After lunch, you're scheduled for makeup and a haircut at my salon. Elise is getting the same, so it'll be like a pajama party." Without missing a beat, she added, "Not *those* pajamas, of course."

Several objections sprang to mind. First: "I can't pay for this and neither should you."

"I'm not." Connie put a kettle of water on the stove. "This is a gift from my mom."

"I'll bet you cajoled her into it!" Marta said, then, seeing no alternative, plopped onto the chair. Elise hung back, watching the cousins as if they hailed from an alien planet.

"Your much-too-stingy aunt Anna is rolling in money, loves to shop and has overlooked her niece for years," Connie responded. "Her only request is before-and-after photos." From her purse, she removed a digital camera and, ignoring Marta's glare, snapped what had to be the world's most unflattering shot.

"Delete that!"

"Don't be ridiculous. It'll give Mom a thrill to see the tremendous improvement in your appearance." Connie eyed the display on the back of the camera. "That *is* disgusting."

"You're shameless!" Marta declared between mouthfuls of cereal. "Anyway, I can't go because I'm tutoring this afternoon."

"Yolanda postponed it to four o'clock, which leaves plenty of time," Connie advised. "She agrees with our plan completely."

Unbelievable. Marta's life had turned into a runaway train.

"I appreciate your letting me tag along," Elise added. "I could use advice from both of you. It's been ages since I paid attention to my appearance."

The desire to argue warred with compassion. Since nothing short of an earthquake would dissuade Connie, and possibly not even that, Marta switched her attention to their friend.

"If I had half your sex appeal, Elise, I'd be thrilled," she confessed. "Put on a provocative outfit and guys will follow you around with their tongues hanging out."

Elise crossed her arms. "I don't want guys following me around, and I'd rather not imagine their tongues hanging out."

Belatedly Marta recalled her mentioning that that had been precisely her problem in high school. No wonder Elise preferred jeans and sweats.

Connie poured hot water into mugs and fixed two instant coffees. "There *is* such a thing as a happy medium," she said as she found a tea bag for Marta.

"That's why I'm counting on you both." Elise stirred sweetener into her drink. "I can't figure out what would be Dr. Federov's style. I mean, Mike's. Don't you think he's cute?" she added.

"Adorable," Connie seconded. "A good man and great with kids."

"What are your plans for the evening?" Marta asked, grateful to see her cousin focus on someone else.

"He's cooking dinner at his condo. The guy's a gourmet," Elise enthused. "He claims he developed an interest in cuisine out of self-defense. He's a vegetarian and it's hard to find good restaurants."

"Sounds like you two had quite a chat after the auction," Connie noted.

"We went out for a drink. Oh, and he invited me to a party with friends after dinner tonight. A small group of professional people, not the kind of crazy bash Hale throws." More tactfully, Elise amended, "I mean, used to throw. Any ideas about what I should wear?"

Connie had a ready answer. "A tailored look. Subdued but stylish. With your wow factor, you can underplay to great effect."

Elise blinked. "I have a wow factor?"

"For sure!" Marta declared. "Wish *I* did." Marta regretted

the words the second they were out of her mouth. She'd played right into her cousin's manicured hands.

"My point precisely!" Connie cleared the dishes. "Go put on something that's easy to take off." Catching a startled glance, she explained, "I mean while trying on clothes. I'm not suggesting you practice seduction techniques. Although that isn't a bad idea."

"It's a terrible idea. I'm not one of those women who fawn all over Derek!" Marta hurried to the section of her studio partitioned as a bedroom. Thank goodness it had a door, even though a two-foot gap remained between the top and the ceiling.

She relished her privacy. This, she feared, was the last she'd have for the rest of the day.

EARLY CHRISTMAS SHOPPING ranked near the bottom of Derek's list of favorite things to do. Two years ago he'd tried to skirt the whole issue by ordering gifts online, but the stuff hadn't looked nearly as appealing in reality as on the Internet. The following year's gift certificates, while practical, hadn't drawn the enthusiasm the rest of his family gave the wrapped items.

He'd like to do better this year, so he headed for the mall on Saturday morning full of good intentions. He rated his chances of success, however, as slim.

Derek always felt at a loss at family events, and this Christmas was likely to be worse than usual. His sister, Jill, married a little over a year, had delivered a baby girl two months ago.

During his visit to the hospital, Derek had struggled to find the right words. His most frequent comment had been, "Yes, she is," spoken whenever someone complimented the baby.

The last thing he needed this holiday was to arrive with stuff as inappropriate as the soccer ball he'd taken to the hospital. "Well, she'll use it later, won't she?" he'd remarked, drawing a long-suffering sigh from his mother and an indulgent head shake from his brother, Tom.

An attorney in the public defender's office, Tom had

chosen his gift at the baby shop where Jill was registered. Derek hadn't even realized stores provided that service for new parents.

By Christmas, little Minnie would be too old for infant items. Surely a good-hearted uncle ought to be able to find *something* suitable. Derek liked kids well enough. He just wasn't accustomed to being around those too small to frame a coherent sentence.

He started this morning's expedition at a toy store. The display of dolls impressed him, but his sister had once claimed they were sexist. A stuffed animal might be better, except that he'd seen a zillion of them in Jill's hospital room.

Discouraged, he suspended that part of his search and prowled through a department store for items that might suit his parents and siblings. A crystal bowl for Mom? The latest kitchen device for Jill? A power tool for Dad or Tom?

Everything seemed generic and predictable. He could never guess what was in their minds, probably because he didn't spend much time with them.

Yet that didn't prevent his family from hitting the mark with Derek. The year he bought his condo, they'd stocked his kitchen with utensils and pots, which he still used. Once, they'd pooled their money to buy him a pair of season tickets to the Angels baseball games. Definitely a home run in the gift category.

This year, though, they weren't likely to score with a sub-scription to a medical journal or new book about Parkinson's research, because he hadn't mentioned his diagnosis. Didn't intend to until he got a lot worse, either.

Setting aside negative thoughts, Derek browsed through more shops, hoping an idea would strike. When that failed, he headed for a bookstore to pick out children's classics and, for the adults, volumes on history and film. They could always exchange the items.

On his way past a ladies' boutique, a familiar face inside

caught Derek's attention. Marta emerged from the dressing room wearing a wine-red dress with ribbons edging the neckline. She swirled in front of a mirror, showing the garment to Connie.

Perhaps Marta's newfound air of sensuality derived from the flattering color or from the ribbons crossing her bosom. Whatever the cause, he flashed back to the softness of her skin and the enticing floral scent as she'd helped him try on costumes.

She's going to have an absolutely fabulous experience. Comprende?

Ruefully, Derek recalled his plan to treat tonight as a casual outing. Scratch that idea. A woman wearing such a sexy dress deserved something special.

He hurried to the bookstore to finish his task. Then he was free to figure out how to indulge his very alluring date.

Chapter Six

Marta hadn't expected to fall in love with a dress. Most outfits left her feeling too short or too round. This claret-hued design brought out a femininity that seemed to belong to someone else, someone more passionate than her practical gift-shop manager persona and far more sophisticated than she'd been in the days when she used to date.

"It's too expensive," she told Connie.

"Don't be silly. When's the last time Mom bought you a gift?" her cousin scoffed.

"She doesn't owe me anything." Marta regarded the price tag in dismay.

"You only think that way because you've been brainwashed by your cheapskate father!" Connie said. "He treats you like some poor relation. Tell me, quick—what did he give you for Christmas last year?"

"Dad doesn't believe in presents for adults." Even a gift certificate to a discount store would have helped Marta's strained budget.

"What did he give Aunt Bling?" Connie pressed.

"A trip to Hawaii." She declined to mention her suspicion that he'd purchased more than a lei for her stepmother as well. "But she's his wife. That's different."

"What did my mother give you before she flew off to New York for a shopping spree?"

"She sent a card. It was lovely!" Marta hadn't expected more from her relatives, although the fact that they'd left town for the holiday had hurt a little. She and Connie had served a charity dinner, then eaten a turkey meal catered by a supermarket deli. After working her shift, Rachel had joined them in watching a hilarious DVD.

"Exactly. You're overdue." Connie shook her head at Elise, who emerged from a dressing chamber in black jeans and a metal-studded jacket. "What do you think you're doing?"

"I like it," their friend said defensively.

Connie thrust a pink-and-gray plaid skirt, gray jacket and pink shell at her. "These! Now!"

"Yes, ma'am." Elise ducked inside.

Later, shopping bags at their sides, they lunched at the food court and drove to the salon. Although instinct urged Marta to insist on a simple trim for her shoulder-length brown locks, she didn't dare risk her cousin's wrath.

She shut her eyes and tried to ignore the smell of chemicals. The snip of scissors. The whir of the dryer.

No matter what they did to her hair, it should eventually grow out. As for Derek, he wasn't likely to notice the change.

But a traitorous part of her hoped he would.

WHEN THE DOOR to Marta's apartment opened, Derek silently thanked his stars he'd glimpsed her dress earlier or he might have dropped his cool demeanor. And that would have been a shame, because he'd put a lot of effort into preparing to play the suave man-about-town. Black suit, his favorite aftershave lotion and a bouquet of roses for his lady.

He forgot all that in an instant. The deep red of Marta's dress brought out a glow in her skin and russet highlights in her hair. Some wizard had changed her style to a layered cut that emphasized her green eyes.

He'd intended to execute a slight bow as he presented the

flowers. Instead, he stood gaping for several seconds before blurting, "You look great!"

"Really?" She seemed in doubt. "Connie said we're going to a steak-and-seafood place. I'm not overdressed, am I?"

The new Mrs. Crandall had designated a popular local restaurant. Derek chose to ignore her recommendation. "I have a surprise, a favorite hideaway I haven't visited in a long while. You'll love it."

"I'm sure I will. What beautiful flowers!" She indicated the bouquet, which he'd forgotten he was holding. "I'd better put those in water."

"Oh. Right!" He thrust them at her, recovering his poise a split second too late. What had happened to his blasé demeanor?

She inhaled deeply and peeked up at him, dark lashes sweeping above the lush blossoms. Then, as if unaware of the effect she'd created, she whirled off.

Feeling light-headed, Derek eased into the apartment, a modest place filled with warmth and color. Ahead in the kitchen, a poster of a mountain meadow expanded the cramped space. To his left, above the couch, three swirling photos of modern dancers contributed movement. At the rear, a partition with a gap at the top revealed an apple-green accent wall.

Marta emerged with a terra-cotta vase, which she set carefully on a side table. "I'll enjoy these."

Although Derek had given any number of arrangements to attractive women, he'd always considered them impersonal, like a box of candy. Not in Marta's apartment. "I wish I'd picked wildflowers," he said impulsively. "Gathered them in a field, like in your poster."

She clasped her hands. "You'd better be careful or I might start believing this is a real date."

The reminder that this *wasn't* a date in the conventional sense jolted him. Derek didn't have designs on Marta. He'd better keep that in mind.

"When exactly is your birthday?" He held the door for her. "I won't be so rude as to ask your age."

After draping a cape over her shoulders, she preceded him outside. The first-floor unit opened onto a concrete walkway level with the yard. "Tomorrow. I'll be thirty-one. It's no secret."

As he locked up with her key, Derek remembered a line he'd rehearsed. Might as well stick to the script. "Tonight, forget about police stations and gift shops and bachelor auctions. Tonight, let me weave a spell."

"That isn't your real self talking," she complained.

"It's your humble servant demonstrating his skill as a ladies' man," he agreed. "Hey, you're entitled to the grand tour, Marta."

"Because Connie and Rachel paid for it?" she asked.

"Because that's who I am." At least for tonight. In fact, he was eager to share this other self with her instead of grumpy everyday Sergeant Reed.

"You can be yourself," she told him a little sadly. "I'm not one of those women who chase you."

Charmed by her earnestness, Derek caught her shoulders and faced her. "I'd have been glad to take you out tonight without the auction. You're my friend, Marta."

"Which is why you don't have to pretend to weave a spell," she shot back. "It isn't necessary."

"It's fun. A game. If you don't mind playing on the same team." He waited for her reaction.

A small nod. "As long as we're in this together."

"The truth is, I've been looking forward to our date," he told her. "We should have done this a long time ago."

He could see that his comment hit the mark. "Then what are we waiting for?"

Derek guided Marta to his car with one palm at the small of her back. Touching and protecting her.

When they reached the sedan, he held the door and extended

the seat belt so she didn't have to stretch for it. He liked tucking her inside, his little Cinderella on her way to the ball.

Amused by his fanciful reflections, Derek circled the carriage and gripped the reins. The wheel. Whatever.

Who cared if the horses were actually a three-hundred-horsepower engine? At least it wouldn't turn into a team of mice at the stroke of midnight.

As for Prince Charming, Derek had never tried to claim that title. But for one evening, he might make an exception.

MARTA HAD OFTEN wondered what a date with Derek would be like. She hadn't expected this, for sure.

A Middle Eastern restaurant with soft, exotic music. Low round tables and the scent of incense. A waiter in what could have passed for an Aladdin costume: white turban, gold-trimmed black vest, black pantaloons gathered at the ankle and a mock scimitar fixed at the waist.

"How authentic is this?" she asked after the man had presented their scroll-style menus and departed.

"About as authentic as Disneyland, I'm guessing." On the semicircular cushioned bench, Derek sat tantalizingly close. A thin curtain sheltered them from the other diners. "How do you like it?"

"I don't usually eat this kind of food." Although she recognized a couple of items on the menu, most of the dishes were unfamiliar. "I'm sure it's fabulous."

"Let's order a sampler for two."

"Great!" She shifted on her pillow. They'd lowered themselves almost to the floor, a position that might have been comfortable had Marta not spent an hour this afternoon with a six-year-old in her lap. The boy had been too restless to sit at a table, so she'd settled him in her lap to review letters and numbers aloud from the safety of her arms. As a result, Marta had a kink in her back.

She refused to let that ruin her evening. Tonight, she

intended to store up memories, from the rumble of Derek's voice to the intoxicating quirk of his smile. Later, she'd review and relish each moment like gems from a treasure chest.

The waiter returned with a selection of dips—hummus, tzatziki and babaghanouj—and a basket of fresh pita. When Derek tore off a piece, scooped up some hummus with it and held the morsel only inches from Marta's lips, she caught his wrist and brought it the rest of the way.

Daringly, she nibbled the edge of his forefinger, where a bit of hummus clung, before releasing him. Marta wasn't sure where she found the nerve.

"My, my," he murmured. "The lady's getting frisky."

She grinned. "You taste pretty good."

"How about you?" Before Marta could react, he leaned toward her and grazed the corner of her mouth with his lips.

Fast and quick, the kiss sent liquid pleasure through her. She tried not to show her reaction as he withdrew, but she wanted more. "No wonder they call you Sergeant Hit-and-Run."

"Too fast?"

"The breeze gave me a chill," Marta retorted.

"Let's see if we can add a little heat." His mouth touched hers again, exploring gently. The flick of his tongue warmed her to the core. "Better?" he asked a bit breathlessly.

"I'll consider that a down payment." She must be out of her mind. But the sensations simmering through her demanded further exploration.

The tempo and volume of the music seemed to increase. For a moment, Marta thought she was imagining the change, but then, through the gauze drapery, she glimpsed a dark-haired woman undulating from a passageway across the room.

Finger cymbals ching-chinged as the dancer's belly performed a series of sexy undulations. A purple-sequined bra highlighted ample breasts, and below the bare midriff, a veil-like skirt swayed on her hips.

Forget skinny fashion models and teenage pop princesses;

this image of seduction bore her womanly curves and forty-plus years with pride. She rippled a path from one table to the next, apparently reveling in her dance. A tiny smile curved her lips when Derek, following custom, tucked a bill into her waistband.

"Lucky lady. He's a sexy sergeant," she observed to Marta before shimmying away.

Suffused with a pleasant buzz, Marta found the comment funny. "Haven't been here in a long while, huh?"

Derek responded with a chuckle. "It *seemed* like a long while."

At a nearby table, a balding man tried to fold money into the dancer's skirt but missed. As he reached again, her hips gave a series of shakes that foiled his efforts, to the amusement of his fellow diners. At last, eyeing the man playfully, she braked to a halt and allowed him to complete the task.

"I can't imagine doing that," Marta admitted. "Feeling so comfortable with your body that you can play like that. And in public!"

Derek's hand cupped hers. "I hope this doesn't feel awkward. I could have chosen a more conventional restaurant."

She hadn't meant her comment that way. "Of course not!" Marta leaned against his shoulder, her cheek brushing the soft fabric of his suit. "I'm enjoying this."

"So am I." Slipping an arm around her waist, he nuzzled her hair. A tantalizing sensation spread through her like wine. Marta had to struggle to remember that they were merely playing a game.

She didn't realize she'd scrunched her nose until he asked, "Am I getting too familiar?"

"Quite the opposite." She sighed. "You certainly live up to my expectations."

"Which expectations would those be?"

"As a lady-killer extraordinaire." Marta hated to admit being as susceptible as any of his other admirers. "Don't expect me to keel over. I might act a little breathless, that's all."

"I'm trained in mouth-to-mouth resuscitation," he murmured. "You'd have to lie down first, though."

"That might muss my new hairdo," Marta returned. "Connie went to a lot of trouble to glam me up. Like it?"

She refrained from mentioning the makeup, although she was pleased that the beautician had managed to conceal the worst of her scars. Marta had bought a bottle of the foundation for future occasions.

Derek studied her approvingly. "You're always appealing, but tonight you glow. I don't think your cousin deserves all the credit."

Unsure how to respond, Marta hurried on, talking to hide her nervousness. "Connie helped me pick the dress. She's got a keen eye, which she doesn't even need. My cousin's a lethal weapon where men are concerned."

"She certainly did a number on Hale," Derek agreed.

"If only I looked more like—" Marta halted. "Don't say a word. I'm not fishing for compliments."

"Good. Because your cousin's not my type," he said.

What is *your type?* Marta choked back the words rather than give him an excuse to rave about exotic brunettes or statuesque redheads. "She's too bossy?" she ventured instead.

"She just doesn't have the same effect on me that you do. I never thought about why."

He might actually choose her over a woman like Connie? But surely he meant as a friend. "We're on the same wavelength. Which is odd, considering that we're such opposites."

"They say opposites attract. Or distract." He adjusted his legs to a different angle beneath the low table. "I must be getting old. Dining this way doesn't feel nearly as comfortable as it used to."

She stretched, too, then told him about holding the six-year-old in her lap. "It's a wonder I managed to drive home."

"You enjoy tutoring enough to endure that?" Quickly, he clarified, "I realize volunteering isn't something you do for amusement. Still, I'd think it'd grow stale after a few sessions."

"Watching a child discover the magic of reading is a thrill that beats anything I can imagine." Since he seemed interested, she went on to talk about her love of teaching and how she could hardly wait to face a whole classroom of her own.

Before she knew it, the waiter arrived with their main course, and after that the meal occupied their attention. The savory meat, stuffed grape leaves and baked eggplant proved delectable.

Derek served as guide, presenting and explaining the dishes with an instinctive sophistication that never seemed affected. He obviously had an interest in fine food and foreign customs.

"Did you travel when you were growing up?" Marta inquired. He rarely mentioned his family.

A head shake. "My most exotic expeditions were to San Francisco, to visit my grandparents. Other than that, establishing his legal career kept Dad busy, and Mom was struggling to finish her law degree." Bitterness underscored his tone. "Frankly, they had no business starting their family so young. I often felt in their way."

"It isn't always a choice," Marta pointed out. "Maybe they didn't plan you."

A pucker formed between Derek's eyebrows. "Perhaps you're right. That hadn't occurred to me."

"They got lucky. You must have been a sweet child." He had so many wonderful qualities.

"Me? I threw tantrums and turned the terrible twos into a three-year rampage," Derek replied ruefully. "When I was five, they had my brother, and at eight my sister joined us. The four of them were compatible and cozy. I never fit in."

"I'll bet they adore you," Marta protested. "No matter how many children I had, each one would be precious."

He reached across to brush a strand of hair from her temple. "That's because you have a generous heart. My grandparents, Mom's folks, were like that."

"And your parents weren't?"

"Like I said, they had more important things to do than deal with my bad behavior." After offering her the stuffed grape leaves, he took a second helping.

"You were only a kid! Parents have to be prepared to deal with occasional misbehavior."

"Occasional? Hardly," he scoffed. "All through school I got in fights and ticked off my teachers. Smart-mouthed my parents, too."

"Really?" She had trouble visualizing that side of Derek.

"I got expelled for fighting during my sophomore year in high school. My parents shipped me off to Grandma and Grandpa. For my own good, but I suspect they were glad to get rid of me." He stared into the distance.

"They probably missed you like crazy!"

"They missed me the way you'd miss a headache," he insisted. "Life at home with my easygoing brother and sister must have been paradise."

"How long were you gone?" Marta asked.

"The rest of the school year." He frowned at the memory. "I did some growing up while I was away, stopped rebelling, but I also gave up any hope of winning my parents' love."

"I didn't mean to stir painful memories." He looked so sad that Marta wished she dared hug him.

"They aren't painful. Not around you." He surveyed their empty plates. "Ready for dessert?"

"I'm not sure I've got any room." Another kiss was what she really wanted.

"Let's find out." He signaled the waiter, who cleared their table and brought a plate of the crispy, honey-drenched pastries called baklava. A single birthday candle glimmered atop one piece. The waiter withdrew, taking their thanks with him.

"How delightful!" Marta inhaled the fragrance. "You ordered this in advance, didn't you?"

"Of course. Prepare for sticky fingers," he warned. "But first, you have to make a wish."

She shut her eyes, and realized that her longtime wish had already been granted: a date with Derek. Her second was impossible: *for him to love me*.

A compromise instead: "I wish for us to be friends always." She blew out the candle.

Derek shook his head. "You aren't supposed to say it aloud."

Oops. "Does that mean it won't happen?"

"I'm granting an emergency dispensation. But only if you let me whisper magic words in your ear." When she agreed, he traced his finger around the shell of her ear.

Desire twisted through Marta. "Those aren't magic words!" she protested.

"I'm not finished." He kissed her lobe, and then murmured a word that sounded like, "Darling."

"What?" She couldn't have heard correctly.

"You look darling in that dress. There. Now your wish will come true. Friends for eternity." He reached for another piece of baklava as coolly as if nothing had passed between them. Which, from his perspective, might be true.

Marta needed to gather her wits. "I'd better wash up." She scooted out of her seat and hurried in search of the ladies' room.

Alone in the tiled chamber, she stared into the mirror. Her skin prickled and her whole body throbbed with heightened sensitivity. She ought to retreat. Call it a night. Thank the man of her dreams and slip away before this celebration got out of control.

Derek's behavior with her was probably the way he acted around every woman he dated. She didn't dare continue this interplay much longer.

After rejoining Derek at the table, Marta reminded him of her earlier comment about the tutoring session. "I've got a major backache. My ibuprofen isn't doing the trick. I'd better go home and soak in the tub."

"It's barely nine o'clock. Your cousin would kill me. Hold on. We'll discuss this in a minute." Derek paid for dinner, sent his compliments to the chef and escorted Marta outside.

A cool night wind brought the fragrance of jasmine coupled with the earthy smell of autumn. Despite her resolve, Marta nestled against the man as they walked to his car. His arm was around her shoulders and his frame sheltered her from the wind.

She hated to move away, but did as Derek clicked open his car and held the door for her.

When they were both inside, snug against the chill air, he said, "I'm the guy who picked the world's most uncomfortable seating arrangement. So I owe you."

"No, you don't. I loved the restaurant." It had been a memorable meal.

"Here's the plan," Derek continued. "We'll swing by your place and pick up a swimsuit. Then we can dissolve our kinks in the hot tub at my complex."

He dropped the remark as if hot tubbing was a natural progression of their activities. Her, Derek and an enveloping cloud of steam. Bad idea.

"I don't wear swimsuits." By way of clarification, Marta noted, "Not the conventional kind."

"What do you wear at the beach?" he asked.

"Exercise shorts and a dark T-shirt."

"Fine. We'll collect your Victorian bathing costume and have a soak. My muscles are a bit tight too, so you'll be doing me a favor. I was afraid you'd prefer dancing and I'm not up for that." He glanced in her direction. "Okay?"

"I…I don't know. People might…" She couldn't complete the sentence. Finally she settled for, "Call me old-fashioned."

"The spa's out in the open. Nothing secluded about it," Derek countered. "Honestly, Marta, I'm not eager for the evening to end. I enjoy your company."

The compliment broke down the last of her defenses. Besides, the water jets might be good for her. "Oh, why not."

"Right decision." He flexed his shoulders. "You're not still worried about your hair, are you?"

"It served its purpose. I can go back to normal now."

"Normal suits me fine," Derek said.

She studied his profile against the passing streetlights. She couldn't believe he'd actually kissed her tonight. And licked her ear. Unbelievable.

Of course, she didn't intend to confess any of that to her friends. It was her secret to treasure.

Just as the rest of the evening would be. Especially the hot tub.

Chapter Seven

Derek supposed he shouldn't have pressured Marta into continuing their date, but her personality energized and tantalized him. He longed for more.

Besides, nobody ought to sit home alone on a Saturday night, especially not someone as cute as Marta. She underestimated herself if she assumed that a guy wouldn't choose to soothe away her aches and pains rather than lose her companionship.

He didn't see her swim outfit when she emerged from her apartment because she'd thrown jeans and a sweater over it. When she stepped from his downstairs powder room without the covering garments, however, he issued an admiring whistle.

The shorts and tee emphasized quite respectable curves. Well, *respectable* might not be the best word.

"Honestly!" Marta sounded indignant. "This is ugly."

"Reminds me of a girls phys-ed class in high school," Derek deadpanned.

"Just the impression a grown woman hopes to give!" She stopped and stared at him. "Hey! Look at you!"

He'd pulled on a pair of dark blue trunks that left his torso bare except for the towel slung over one shoulder. Now he felt her appreciative gaze roaming over his lightly tanned chest and legs.

"Like the picture?" Derek prodded.

"I'm not blind," Marta returned smartly. "You live up to your billing, Sarge."

"Worth the purchase price?"

"Every penny. Of course, it wasn't my money." When he handed her a towel, she draped it around her neck. "Lead on."

"This way." He took her through the kitchen and garage, where a side door from the laundry area ushered them onto a walkway.

Nippy air hastened what might have been a leisurely stroll between beds of flowering bushes and low, fat palms. Pop music drifted from one condo; from another, the sounds of a TV program.

Derek unlocked the gate to the pool area, which was currently unoccupied. Illuminated from within, the spa sent wisps of steam into the darkness.

They dropped their towels on the concrete. Marta hurried to slide into the water, and as she sank onto one of the benches, her expression registered pure bliss. Derek smiled. It felt good to make her happy.

He joined her in the pool. "Too bad we have to wear clothes in here," he murmured as warmth penetrated his body.

She eyed him skeptically. "Are you flirting with me?"

"I don't think so." Derek feigned innocence.

"Inducing a woman to remove her clothes hardly counts as flirting," Marta mused. "It's more of an obvious play."

That stung. "I'm never obvious."

Her fingers waggled amid the bubbles. "Don't worry. I'm confident that you have no designs on my body."

True, except for a small corner of his mind that urged him onward. "What makes you so sure?"

"Well—" mischief danced through her voice "—at your advanced age, you'll probably have trouble climbing out of the hot tub, let alone behaving like a stallion afterward."

He drifted toward her on the bench and reached out to tickle her midriff. "That sounds like a challenge."

Giggling, Marta squirmed away. "How you gonna catch me, Grandpa?"

"You can't escape in a spa!"

They struggled in play, laughing and splashing. To Derek's pleasure, Marta didn't try to disguise how much she was enjoying their interaction. And in the warm water, as his hard body grazed her soft one, Derek became increasingly aware of his attraction to her. Her vitality thrilled him; her lushness excited him.

At last, he pulled her closer until she relaxed against him, legs tangling with his. So tempting. So delightful.

As a token of victory, he kissed her. With a sigh, she opened to him, her lips and tongue meeting his. He cradled her and intensified the kiss, half expecting her to pull away with a wisecrack.

Instead, Marta caressed his shoulders and smoothed her palms down his arms. Derek wondered why he hadn't registered before how fiercely they were drawn to each other.

UNBELIEVABLE THAT THIS WAS happening: Derek's hard body giving unmistakable evidence of arousal and his mouth on hers, while his arms encircled her hips. Marta no longer wanted to resist, regardless of the consequences.

For too many years, she'd allowed the accident and her disabilities to define her. She'd never imagined she'd make love to the most desirable man she knew. Never imagined that he'd want it, too. She had to accept that afterward they'd proceed on their separate paths. Perhaps a woman existed who could domesticate this rogue, but it wasn't her. Still, she wasn't going to waste this opportunity, and if she contemplated her decision for too long, she might chicken out.

"You know where this is leading," she murmured.

Derek stopped tracing a finger down her T-shirt toward the vee of her breasts. "That's up to you."

"Okay, but no cracks about my height," she returned levelly.

"Wouldn't dream of it." A slightly amused note.

"I'd better warn you," Marta added.

"Of what?"

"First, I wasn't kidding about the scars." The prospect of revealing them still scared her.

"I'll kiss each one." He raised her palm to his mouth and pressed his lips to it, as if in demonstration.

The gesture raised a delicious shiver. "Okay. But afterward… we'll be friends again. No romantic illusions."

That seemed to give Derek pause. Briefly, anyway. At last: "Fine with me. I'm not good at relationships. If we can keep it light…"

"Light, and out of the bedroom," she clarified, in case he expected more. "It's a one-time deal." Had to be. Otherwise, she might fall far too deeply in love.

"Birthday present?" he murmured.

"Exactly." She smiled.

"I'll do my best to make it one you'll never forget." He sounded utterly sincere.

Marta smiled. "That shouldn't be a problem."

"I certainly hope not."

Had she imagined a hint of uncertainty in his response? About to inquire further, she gave a start as the creaky pool gate announced the arrival of company. Childish squeals dispelled any hope that the newcomers might be another amorous couple or a solo night swimmer.

The two of them climbed out of the hot tub, gathered their towels and headed toward the condo. Despite the cool air on their wet bodies, Marta didn't mind the stroll, as long as Derek's hand possessed hers.

She savored the awareness crackling between them. Every touch that must seem commonplace to other lovers—a halt outside his unit as he kissed her again; drying each other in the garage so they didn't track water through the kitchen—felt special.

They only had this once. *Until the stroke of midnight.* Not literally, but the phrase seemed apt.

They left their towels on the washing machine and went upstairs together. On the staircase, Derek positioned her above him so their mouths met at the same level. His thumbs probed her nipples, arousing such intense sensations that Marta gasped. When he brought his mouth to the hard points of her breasts, fire seared through her.

Derek lifted his head. "We'd better move into the bedroom before this happens right here. You'd get a permanent crick in your spine."

"Besides," she reminded him, "you promised to kiss each of my scars, and that'll keep you busy for hours."

"Little imp," he returned fondly. "Did I mention I have a few scars of my own for you to explore? They're in extremely interesting places."

"I can't wait."

In the king-size bed, they showed each other their scars. Derek went first, revealing the residue of a gunshot wound to the ribs that he'd received early in his career. He also pointed out the thin remnant of a knife fight along his inner thigh. It had led to his departure from high school and subsequent removal to San Francisco, he explained. "The other guy started it. A bully who objected to my defending his victims."

"What happened to him?" Marta asked.

"Got sent to juvenile hall." Derek shrugged. "At least the other kids didn't have to suffer his nastiness during my absence."

"Did you see him after that?"

"No. Good thing, because I'd have fought him again if necessary. Still, he helped me decide to become a police officer. There are a lot of bullies in the world, and a lot of folks who need protecting."

He fixed his attention on her. "Now, let's see what you've been so embarrassed about."

Despite Marta's bravado, she shrank from having her imperfections scrutinized, especially by this man who had his pick of lovely women.

She struggled against the urge to yank the bedspread across herself. "Why don't you turn off the light?"

"Relax." Gently, Derek raised her shirt and cupped her breasts. Hot with yearning, Marta arched slightly as he proceeded to tug off her shorts. But the sense of anticipation faded fast.

She could visualize all too well the picture spread before his gaze, the web of incisions across her hips and thighs from the crash and from surgeries to repair shattered bones. When she'd first glimpsed her damaged body in a mirror, she'd wept.

Derek touched his mouth to her left leg above the knee. She lay motionless as he followed the scar higher, then traced a second scar and a third.

When he transferred his attention to her vulnerable core, the last trace of embarrassment vanished, replaced by sheer longing. Marta forgot her inhibitions as he removed her panties and his trunks.

She remembered the need for precautions. "Shouldn't we…?"

"Yes. In a minute." Derek rose above her, his ridge pressing her most yielding point. "Sure you're ready?"

She reached up to caress the line of his jaw. "Yes."

Their mouths met, but Derek hesitated. She didn't understand why, unless he'd stopped to put on protection. But he simply balanced there, immobile.

A second later, she discovered the problem. He'd lost some of that rigidity.

"Damn," he muttered.

Failure to perform? She hadn't expected that of Derek. But then, any guy could have problems, she knew.

He rolled over and lay with his back to Marta. When she touched him, she felt him tense.

"Those darn hot tubs," she said. "They get you all excited and wring you out at the same time."

"Guess that's it. Sorry to let you down."

"No fair hogging the blame." She massaged the taut muscles between his shoulder blades. "I've been out of the game for over ten years. Maybe if I knew the right moves, this wouldn't have happened."

"No, it isn't your fault." Turning to face Marta, he touched her cheek. "You look cute naked."

"No, I don't."

"Hey, who's the expert here?" he said.

"Okay, I yield." She ran her palm over his stomach. "You must lift weights. You're like a rock down there."

"Wish that were true." Spoken ruefully.

Her hand moved lower, daring to touch him. Then, with a boldness she hadn't suspected she possessed, her mouth followed.

A groan ripped from Derek's throat. For a while, he lay still as Marta tantalized him into readiness, and then he took over. Flipped her to lie beneath him. Nuzzled her and, poised above, joined them with a thrust.

Waves of pleasure washed over Marta, and she wrapped her legs around him. At the periphery of her awareness, she recalled that they ought to wait, ought to stop and put on protection, but a self she'd almost forgotten had sprung into life, and there was only now, these moments of exquisite pleasure.

Every inch of her pulsated with sensation as Derek's pace quickened, and when he cried out his release, a burst of white light transported Marta beyond her ordinary being. The edges of old wounds drew shut, deep-seated fissures healed, and the last of her psychic injuries vanished into elation.

She clung to Derek. Without him as anchor, she feared her molecules might scatter across the universe.

Only as the heat dissipated did she register what a wonderful and scary thing had just happened. She'd given Derek a piece of her soul. What she'd experienced transcended physical love.

But she'd known the rules when they started. Somehow, despite this sense of rightness, she had to let him go.

HE UNDERSTOOD AT LAST what he'd been waiting for these past months of self-imposed isolation: desire coupled with trust. For the security of being with a woman who wouldn't judge or reject.

Derek held Marta beneath the covers, savoring the last embers of lovemaking. If only they could continue this way for weeks or months, until their passion waned. "Change your mind?" he inquired.

Sleepily, she rubbed her cheek against his chest. "About what?"

"A return match," he explained. "We're lovers. Might as well play it out."

He could have phrased that more romantically, Derek supposed. But he had no intention of trying to fool Marta into believing he might become the kind of steady, reliable guy she deserved.

"You're not getting rid of me that way." Slipping from his grasp, she raised herself on one elbow.

"Excuse me?"

"I'm onto you, Sarge," Marta replied tartly. "We had fun in the sack so now you're ready to stick me in column A—temporary playmate. Satisfying your masculine urges until we exhaust each other, or until I get clingy and whiny. Then you say sayonara."

"Unfair," he protested, although she was right.

"Eat your heart out." Throwing off the covers, she scooted out of bed. "I've been dying to try your bathtub ever since Thursday. You can shower or not, but once I'm presentable, you're driving me home."

"Already?" He'd never had a woman essentially kick *him* out of bed before.

"We have a deal," Marta reminded him. "That includes staying friends. *Somebody* has to sell you snacks at the hospital and set you straight when you get full of yourself. Go ahead, shed a few tears into the pillow, but eventually you'll thank me."

With those words, she collected her wet clothes and whisked out of sight. A moment later, she called, "You can fetch my jeans and sweater when you bring my glass of wine."

Derek had to laugh at her audacity. He'd quit stocking alcohol at his doctor's suggestion, however. "How about grape juice?"

"Sure. Or a hot toddy. Isn't that what people used to drink when you were young?" she taunted through the door.

"Watch out, wench, or I'll come in there for an instant replay."

"Promises, promises!"

He couldn't pass up the chance for what might be their last intimate encounter. This time, Derek remembered to bring a condom. The odds of encountering problems from one mistake were small, but he saw no sense in pushing his luck.

"SURE, WE SLEPT TOGETHER!"

Elise beamed at the trio of riveted young women around the restaurant table. She'd been regaling them with details of her evening with Mike Federov, from the vegetable lasagna he'd fixed to their dancing in his living room to the sophisticated music of Michael Bublé. Rachel had braved an indiscreet question, which Elise had just cheerfully answered.

Until her friend conveniently took the spotlight, Marta had worried about how to keep from revealing too much of her personal adventures last night. She'd been so worried, in fact, that, had this not been her birthday, she might have invented an excuse to postpone the dinner or at least changed the venue from the conversation-friendly China Queen to a noisy pizza place.

Impossible to avoid the topic entirely, of course. On arrival, Marta had sketched her adventures with Derek in a lighthearted vein, omitting any hint of mind-blowing sex. She'd then shifted the focus to Elise, who had more than risen to the occasion. According to her, the child psychologist possessed not only great prowess in bed but also the patience of a saint and the wisdom of Solomon.

"He actually listens to what I say!" she enthused as the waiter set aromatic platters on the table. As usual, they'd ordered dishes to share: candied walnut shrimp, Mongolian beef, kung pao chicken and sweet-and-sour pork. "He has incredible insights into how to bring up children, too. Can you imagine?"

"Well, yeah." Rachel plopped a clump of steamed rice onto her plate. "That's his specialty."

"I keep fearing there must be a fatal flaw," Elise admitted. "Has Russ mentioned Mike's past involvements? I mean, whether he has a bad record with women?"

"Not that I'm aware of." Rachel rarely took much interest in gossip. "He's a great guy. Here's a word of advice, though—let things develop naturally. I see that 'cuff 'em and book 'em' look in your eye."

"Doesn't work with guys," Connie agreed. "Except for Rachel and Russ, but that was different."

Elise piled a heap of beef and pork onto her plate. "I guess you're right. I'm so excited, I'm likely to chase him away."

Connie measured out a small portion of chicken and kept it separate from the rice. A neat freak, she'd at least relaxed her housekeeping standards since Skip and Hale moved in. Marta used to nurse a sneaking sympathy for Joel, who'd complained during their marriage that he couldn't fix a snack without his wife insisting he sweep the floor afterward.

Diving into her own generous helpings of food provided a welcome cover for Marta's thoughts. She hated keeping secrets from her friends, but her reactions to last night hovered between exhilaration and agony.

Their second lovemaking session had left them both gasping and laughing from the logistical challenges posed by the bathroom. In the shower, on the mat… She beamed at the memory and stuffed a forkful of shrimp in her mouth before having to explain.

"You really love this food," Rachel remarked, misinterpreting her smile. "I'm glad we came here."

"You guys went way beyond the call of duty with that present," Marta added when she'd finished chewing. "I can't believe your husbands let you spend that much."

"It was for charity," Rachel said.

"Hey, my income is my business, as long as I contribute my share to the household," Connie added.

"Isn't it great to meet a man who isn't macho?" Elise chimed in, and segued into yet another anecdote about Mike.

Marta had read in a magazine that love affairs tended to have a honeymoon period, followed by a period of adjustment as the lovers gave free rein to their less endearing traits. She hoped Elise didn't abandon ship at the first sign of water on the deck.

No danger of that in Marta's relationship with Derek. They'd both jumped off while still at full sail. Happy memories of a shipboard romance, and no risk of hitting the rocks.

No chance of sailing into the sunset, either. But the sense of healing remained. Last night's encounter with Derek had restored her self-image as a desirable woman. Perhaps after she earned her degree, she might be ready to look around for a keeper. By then, surely Derek would have quit dominating her thoughts.

"You're glowing," Connie observed. "You honestly expect us to believe that all you and Sergeant Hit-and-Run did was nibble baklava and watch belly dancing?"

Marta couldn't summon a single response that didn't reveal how much she'd enjoyed sex. Mercifully, fate gave her a break as a group of diners vacated a central table and she glimpsed the couple in a booth beyond.

"Can you believe that?" she said. "It's your ex-husband and Tracy!"

Connie, who had her back to the room, measured out a portion of beef. "Big deal. She paid for him."

"She's sitting in his lap!" exclaimed Rachel, usually the most unflappable member of the group.

Startled, Connie craned her neck to look. Elise bumped the table as she angled for a glimpse.

Across the restaurant, the couple remained oblivious. The reporter, her brown hair loose over her shoulders and her skirt bunched high on her thighs, curled against Joel, who wore a goofy grin. Empty dishes in front of them testified that they'd finished dinner and, Marta mused, had started on dessert—the do-it-yourself kind.

"I can't believe it! Joel's usually such a grouch." Of course, Elise dealt with him mostly as a supervisor during her patrol shifts.

"I can't imagine what he's thinking." Connie returned her gaze to her companions. "Or perhaps I should say, what he's thinking *with*. Obviously nothing above the waist."

Rachel poured a second cup of green tea, to which she added two spoonfuls of sugar. "Tracy's more the type to throw herself at a story than a man."

"All the same, there's a girl in there somewhere." Connie signaled to the waiter for more hot water. "She *does* buy my rose-scented soap."

Unwillingly, Marta entertained a less charitable view. Although she wished Tracy and Joel well, perhaps things weren't as they appeared. "I hope he understands she's planning to write about their date."

Dismay greeted this remark. "How awful!" Rachel said.

"Just what the police department needs—more bad press," Elise grumbled.

Connie did a slow burn. "I've had my issues with Joel, but he deserves better treatment."

Marta couldn't believe Tracy would dally with a man sexually in order to exploit him. She felt a bit guilty, too, since she'd recommended Joel as a good subject. And, uncomfortably, she recalled Tracy commenting on his reputation as a controlling male who deserved a comeuppance. "Maybe she intends to leave the fun parts out of her story."

"I wouldn't bet on it," Elise muttered.

At the booth, the couple disentangled and rose to leave. Judging by their snuggling, they didn't plan to go bowling.

"Should we warn him?" Elise asked.

"I could walk by and kind of trip him," Rachel suggested. "Or her."

"Connie, can't you find an excuse to give him a hint?" Marta asked.

Her cousin waggled her fingers in a count-me-out gesture. "I'm the last person he'd listen to."

A troubled silence fell over the table as Joel and Tracy exited with their arms around each other. Marta wondered if she ought to call Derek, as public information officer, and alert him to a possible scandal brewing. Still, his job didn't involve lecturing a lieutenant about proper conduct.

Connie's voice broke into her thoughts. "Also, we're ignoring an important point."

"Which is?" Rachel asked.

"Joel's perfectly aware that she's a reporter. He's not a rookie. Surely he can see the potential for trouble." Connie stopped as the waiter refilled the teapot and their water glasses. When they were alone, she continued, "Perhaps *he* has an agenda."

"Seducing her into going easy on the department?" Elise said. "It's possible."

"Pretty funny if they're both laying traps," Rachel added.

"You're making my head hurt." Marta said. She found intrigue confusing. Although her friends raved about such thrillers as *The Bourne Identity* and *The Da Vinci Code*, she had trouble following the plots.

"Anyway, they're gone," Rachel announced. "Unless

some-body's planning to phone him, I guess we're letting matters run their course."

"I wonder what Mike would say." Elise wasted no time returning to her favorite topic.

For Marta's part, despite her resolve, she itched to call Derek, ostensibly in the interests of the police force but mostly to hear his voice. Recovering from their encounter, she supposed, was like going on a diet. You had to fight the cravings until they subsided.

She intended to do exactly that.

Chapter Eight

On a Thursday morning a few weeks later, Derek arrived at the office early. He liked to scan the weekly paper before heading to his meeting with hospital staff.

During the eight or nine months since launching the prevention sessions, he'd completed a review of major types of symptoms of abuse to watch for. However, as he'd written in a recent update to the chief, he believed the program remained valuable in reinforcing awareness and encouraging the staff to discuss incipient problems.

Derek hadn't mentioned how much he looked forward to seeing Marta at the hospital. In addition, since their lovemaking, he often dropped by between outings to purchase snacks and simply say hello. Just passing through. Touching base. Letting her boost his spirits.

She'd been right about the friendship thing. Derek doubted he'd behave well had the two of them planned a continuing involvement. Getting intimate activated a deep-seated protective mechanism. Well, they were both safe on that score.

He turned his attention to the *Villazon Voice*, scanning the front page. When he first took this post, he'd had a tendency to lose his temper. After completing several training seminars, however, he'd learned to respect the fact that reporters, no matter how obnoxious, were simply doing their job.

This week, Tracy had aimed her guns at the chamber of commerce. The current president was pushing the city council to require business licenses of individuals who worked at home. The reporter had interviewed artists, medical transcribers and a freelance writer, who objected to paying fees when they received no special services and didn't generate traffic.

Good reporting, in Derek's view. A far cry from the story she'd written about her date with Joel.

The main article concerning the auction had portrayed the officers and other bachelors in a positive, if slightly humorous, light. The same couldn't be said of the sidebar headlined "My Night with Lt. Hunk."

Although Tracy hadn't identified the man in the story, anyone who'd attended the auction knew his name. She'd cast Joel as a muscle-bound stereotype who spent his weekends decimating woods and streams. "On the job, Rambo may protect us good guys from the crooks, but when he's hunting, does he spare a thought for the poor little animals?"

At least the woman had omitted any reference to extracurricular activities on her date. Derek gathered from Joel's initial comments that the pair hadn't exactly called it an early night. In any case, while Joel had considered the entire outing off the record, Tracy obviously hadn't. She'd phoned him later, apparently expecting him to treat the story as a joke. According to Joel, he'd informed her that from now on he intended to guard his privacy by staying as far away from her as possible. Thus had ended what, according to Marta's observations of the pair canoodling in a Chinese restaurant, might have been a promising romance.

Luckily for Joel, Chief Lyons had taken the incident well. Still, he'd agreed with Derek's recommendation that they schedule a refresher series of training sessions for watch commanders, desk officers and detectives about coping with the media.

Great. Other cops took down stalkers and armed robbers; Derek provided tips on how to coddle reporters. Not exactly what he'd set out to accomplish when he began this career.

Feeling restless and with time to spare before the hospital gig, he strode down the hall. Although the chief's secretary kept a pot of coffee brewing in her office next door to his, Derek preferred detouring to the lunchroom to soak up the sights and sounds of the station.

At 9:00 a.m., the place lay quiet, unlike the bustle at shift change or the hubbub on a weekend evening when drunk drivers and troublemakers got processed and put into holding cells. The desk officer fiddled with a crossword puzzle, the dispatchers were discussing the plot of their favorite soap opera, and in the watch commander's office, Joel sat with his feet on the desk.

Derek was doctoring his coffee in front of a vending machine when his cell rang. He hadn't given the number to the press, but Tracy had nosed it out, and he recognized her ID.

"What can I do for you?" he asked after they exchanged greetings.

"I understand Allen Jennings got a ticket yesterday on Arches Avenue." Jennings, who starred in a hit TV show, occasionally made the hour drive from Hollywood to visit his mother in Villazon.

"So I hear." Derek had spotted the item in the morning report, in which the night watch commander summarized occurrences to alert the day staff.

"He's raising a fuss. Says nobody gets ticketed on Arches because it's such a busy street with little cross traffic. Claims the cop singled him out because he drives a Ferrari."

"Yeah, our guys hate Ferraris," Derek shot back. "Drive an expensive car in Villazon and you're fair game." Quickly he added, "I meant that facetiously. Don't quote me."

"I do understand sarcasm," Tracy retorted. "Is the department standing by the ticket?"

As Derek recalled, patrolman Bill Norton had clocked the Ferrari at fifteen mph over the speed limit. In addition, the driver had become verbally abusive after being pulled over and initially refused to sign the ticket. Norton had decided against arresting the jerk, which was lucky, since that would have brought in a flock of paparazzi.

Treat celebrities with care or they'll make your life miserable. That had been one of Derek's points in last week's media-training session. However, fame didn't excuse lawbreaking.

"In my opinion, the officer behaved appropriately under the circumstances. Mr. Jennings is no different from any other motorist when he endangers lives." Derek heard the click of computer keys as Tracy transcribed his words. "Are you telling me the guy called you to beef?"

She hesitated. Then: "No. I heard it appeared in the morning report, so I called Jennings's public relations agency for his response."

"Who told you about it?" The morning report was supposed to remain confidential.

"I have my sources. Thanks for your help." She rang off fast.

Derek gritted his teeth at this unsatisfactory response. Their local newshound had an uncanny ability to uncover controversial items involving the Villazon PD. The woman claimed she had a wide circle of acquaintances who kept their ears open, but this had to be an insider. At various times in the past, suspicion had fallen on a records clerk, an Explorer Scout and a garrulous patrolman. All had been exonerated. With half an hour to spare, Derek decided to canvass the most likely pigeon in this instance.

He strolled into Joel's office. Feet still on the desk, the guy sat staring through a glass wall in the direction of the lobby. The newspaper tossed onto a chair indicated he had at least glanced at today's articles. Derek had recommended doing so. *Keep abreast of stories that concern your cases. It's the best way to learn about the media's angles and assumptions.*

Joel glanced up. "What can I do for you?"

Derek leaned in the doorway. "Tracy didn't happen to call today, did she? Pump you for information on the morning report?"

"She knows better than to try to manipulate me again," Joel groused. "I treat her the same as any other reporter, period. On the job, anyway."

This last remark caught Derek's attention. "You two are seeing each other again?"

"She called last week with tickets to a Lakers game. I couldn't let them go to waste, could I? We went and had a great time—they won, so of course I had to take her out for a late dinner." Flippantly, Joel added, "She signed a nondisclosure statement first. Not one word in the paper."

The relationship still sounded risky to Derek. "Did you talk to her this morning?"

"No. Why?"

"Minor leak," Derek said.

"Didn't come from me." Joel sounded irritated. "Anything else on your mind? Some of us have *real* work to do."

Derek swallowed a sharp response about the tough labor involved in staring out the window. Besides, although he resented the slur about his position, he'd never corrected his friend's assumption that he'd requested it as a stepping-stone into administration.

"Yeah, I got nothing better to do. Guess I'll go impress the chicks in white uniforms," he replied dryly. "Catch you later."

Before departing for the Mesa View Medical Center across the street, Derek stopped in to see the desk officer and the traffic sergeant. Neither of them had spoken with Tracy, either. So where the heck did she get her information? Derek mulled over the subject as he gathered his notes on today's topic— elder abuse—and exited the building.

He wished he could devise a more proactive means of ferreting out Tracy's source. As public information officer, he considered the matter his responsibility. And nipping this problem would go a long way toward helping resolve the PD's image problems.

He really cared about his fellow officers. They put their lives on the line on a regular basis, and deserved better than to catch flak for some tiny misstep, real or imagined. He also felt a strong personal loyalty to Will Lyons.

A veteran of the Whittier and Los Angeles police forces, the chief had arrived a year and a half ago with a mission to restore the community's confidence in its men and women in blue. Although his reserved manner made him appear aloof, he often sought ways to support his troops.

In a recent performance review, Will had written that Derek was extremely valuable to the bureau, had praised the PIO's initiative and contended that he'd improved morale. More important, the guy had handled the Parkinson's diagnosis with discretion and tact.

Perhaps, Derek mused, the key to finding the leak lay in using his skills as an investigator. Now he had to figure out where to start snooping.

As Marta adjusted the Thanksgiving decorations she'd posted around the boutique, she mentally reviewed the items she'd culled to amuse Derek. Chief among them was a funny anecdote from the Internet about a pair of burglars who'd hit a convenience store and left a trail of snack wrappers leading to their apartment next door.

Next semester, when she was enrolled in *two* courses, she doubted she'd have time to prepare for his visits. But for now, she relished bringing a smile to his lips. It was one way to hold his interest.

On a purely platonic level, of course.

There he was now, pausing at the hospital entrance as an elderly couple preceded him through the automatic door. Bathed in sunlight, Derek's tall frame stirred memories of tumbled bedsheets and a steamy bathroom.

A perky college-age volunteer intercepted his course as he strode across the lobby. Marta couldn't hear their conversation, but the young woman sparkled.

How wonderful to be so free-spirited, so…unmarred and open to adventure. To still have the illusion that all things were possible. How could a man resist?

Yet Derek gazed past her and signaled Marta with a slight nod. Just a hint of recognition that indicated they shared a special understanding.

An understanding of which kind of candy bar he preferred, she chided herself. Nothing more.

The young woman, whose name tag read Celia, walked with him toward the gift shop. "That's a fascinating subject," she remarked as they came within earshot. "I mean, fascinating in a horrible way. Like, who would abuse the elderly?"

Apparently she'd asked him about today's topic. Although Marta doubted the girl harbored a deep desire to rescue senior citizens, Celia appeared to listen raptly as Derek explained that problems arose both in institutions and in private homes.

He didn't flirt or crack jokes. At least not until he glanced at Marta. "New sweater?" He indicated her cobalt-blue top. "Great color."

Marta smiled and smoothed her hands over the knit, then realized she'd just emphasized the way it clung to her breasts. *Darn.*

"It sure is," Celia chimed in. "You know, if you got plastic surgery for those scars, you'd be very pretty."

The thoughtless remark left Marta speechless.

Derek replied for her. "Some of us consider her very pretty now."

Marta could have hugged him. "Thanks."

Celia's mouth flew open as she recognized her error. "I meant… Gee, I'm sorry."

Marta took pity on her. "That's okay. If I weren't saving my money for tuition, maybe I'd consider it."

"Oh, gosh, I'm such a dolt! Anyway, I'm neglecting my duties." The volunteer indicated the refrigerated glass case. "Do you have flowers for a Mr. Lopez in room 330B? I'm supposed to deliver them."

"Of course." Marta produced the bouquet and vase, which had been ordered and paid for by phone. "Keep the card turned so it's visible, okay?"

"I'll be careful!" Still flustered, the young woman hurried off with the gift.

Derek folded his arms. "You were too kind. You should stick up for yourself."

Marta had no desire to discuss Celia. "Maybe I should keep you around to stick up for me."

"Maybe you should." The serious tone took her aback. Before she could consider its possible significance, however, he switched subjects. "Listen, you might be able to help me with a problem."

"Sure. What?" Providing assistance beat the heck out of trying to entertain him with a silly anecdote, she thought.

Derek rested one arm on the counter. "You must hear a lot of gossip—scratch that—valuable information. At Villa Corazon, in the hospital, or simply with friends."

"I suppose so." Marta attracted confidences, probably because she listened so sympathetically.

"Someone's sneaking Tracy Johnson inside tips about the department," he went on. "I'd like to find out who, because this is hurting us. I'd greatly appreciate your letting me know if you hear anything relevant."

The request startled Marta. "I'm not sure that's appropriate. What if it turned out to be Hale or Rachel? Not that I consider it likely. I couldn't rat on them."

His gaze softened. "Of course not. You're the most loyal person I know."

"No one admires the police more than I do," she persisted, despite the temptation to please him by agreeing. "But if officers are doing stuff they shouldn't, Tracy *ought* to hear about it."

"Agreed. I have no quarrel with Ms. Johnson on that score." To her relief, Derek continued making his case without apparent rancor at her demurral. "Only, I believe whoever's leaking information carries a grudge. This isn't a matter of doing one's civic duty, it's about stabbing fellow officers in the back."

Unwillingly, Marta thought of Elise. Although a few officers had supported her grievance against Vince Borrego, a large segment of the force had treated her like dirt. The cold shoulders and snide remarks, although now consigned to the past, still rankled.

"I'd like to help," Marta said. "But, Derek, I can't. I'd be violating my friends' trust."

She hadn't realized how emotional she felt until tears stung her eyes. No matter how much she longed to win his approval, she couldn't abandon her principles.

"I didn't think of it in that light." He spoke gently. "It's okay, Marta. I don't intend to strong-arm my friends into spying for me."

She swallowed. "You're not mad?"

"Not even a little."

Another point occurred to her. "There is one thing I can tell you because it isn't a secret."

Derek studied her keenly. "I'd be grateful."

"Vince signed up to tutor at the center." Elise was furious, especially since he'd chosen Saturday afternoons. Sure, the center needed volunteers for that busy day, but their schedules overlapped and she loathed having to face him on a regular basis.

"Did he say why?" Derek checked the wall clock. He still had ten minutes, Marta noted. "The man never struck me as the altruistic type."

"He mentioned being a grandfather and also wanting to repay the community for the damage he caused." Vince had seemed sincere, according to Yolanda. Connie and Rachel, also, were giving him the benefit of the doubt. But Marta's sympathies lay with Elise.

"Has he started already?"

"He's begun orientation. His first tutoring session is this weekend, I believe." Another aspect occurred to her. "Ben Lyons seems to spend Saturdays doing chores for the center. He hangs around with Vince a lot. Of course, they *are* neighbors at Yolanda's fourplex."

Derek selected a couple of chocolate bars. "If Borrego is trying to undermine his successor, he's on the right track. Things are touchy enough between Will and his son already."

"You believe Vince is that much of a snake?" Marta asked.

Her choice of words brought a smile. "A snake. Yes, that's exactly the term I'd use. I keep hoping the guy's genuinely reformed. Unlikely, though."

"What are you going to do about it?" she asked. "Since I won't carry tales, I mean."

"Haven't decided." He winked. "Since you're so discreet, you'll be the first person I confide in."

"Promises, promises!" Marta stopped. The phrase summoned tantalizing details of the evening when she'd thrown the same challenge at him for quite different reasons. Remembering the way he'd powered into the bathroom, almost too large for the enclosed space, and pressed her against the wall brought a rush of desire.

He was recalling it, too, she gathered from Derek's sudden intake of breath. His mouth angled toward hers as he moved nearer.

Abruptly, he reached over her head and plucked a helium balloon from its tether. "I'll take this, please."

The balloon read, Kiss Me, I'm a Nurse.

"Who's the lucky girl?" The words stuck in Marta's throat.

"What?" He glanced at the thing. Apparently he hadn't noticed the inscription. He must have grabbed it to cover their near embrace. Otherwise, it would have been obvious to Russ, who'd just walked in.

"Give it to Nora Dellums," she suggested. The ultrasound technician had recently broken up with her boyfriend. "She could use a lift."

"Done." He paid, and turned to greet Rachel's husband. After they exchanged pleasantries, Derek headed for the elevator.

Russ held out change for a roll of breath mints. "I didn't see a thing."

"There was nothing to see," Marta corrected.

"And I saw none of it," he confirmed with a twinkle.

"Good." She took his payment and then, after his departure, bought herself a roll of mints as well. She hoped they'd help settle her stomach, which had been bothering her for several days.

A group of mothers-to-be, arriving for a prenatal tour, flocked into the concession. Amid their exclamations over the stuffed animals and baby gifts, Marta was able to cool the lingering heat of her encounter with Derek.

She'd better watch herself. If they kept tempting each other, she reflected dryly, she'd have to start stocking balloons that said, Kiss Me, I'm an Idiot.

Chapter Nine

"This is stupid." The skinny boy, whose age Derek guessed to be about ten, folded his arms and tilted back his chair. The young woman sitting across the table from him fingered the math book in frustration.

Around them, the auditorium of Villa Corazon hummed with the conversations of students and tutors, some in small groups, others in pairs. Derek had stopped by the office in search of Yolanda Rios, and been directed to the central room. As might be expected on a Saturday afternoon, a sizable group was assembled.

Despite the noise level, the intensity of most participants struck him at once. With few exceptions, the several dozen students appeared determined to master their material.

The exceptions included this boy. To the young woman's comment that math formed the basis of many careers as well as daily activities, he replied, "So what? I won't need it."

The situation was none of his business, Derek supposed. But while speaking at schools on safety and crime prevention, he'd encountered his share of wise guys, and this kid needed an attitude adjustment.

He introduced himself and, after obtaining the volunteer's permission, addressed the student. "Any idea what you expect to do with your life?"

"Yeah." The boy's lip curled. "I'm going to be a drug dealer like my big brother."

The woman gasped. "Tom!"

The response was a smug grin. Although surely the boy didn't understand all the implications of his remark, he'd be old enough in only a few years to fall under the influence of a drug-dealing gang. Even at this age, he might be recruited to serve as a lookout.

"How many pounds in a kilo?" Derek demanded.

Blank expression.

"Two-point-two," he said. "Drugs are weighed in grams and kilograms, in case you didn't know."

Tom shrugged.

"Here's another problem," Derek continued. "Your supplier suggests a three hundred percent markup. What does that mean?"

The boy cleared his throat. No words emerged.

"You'd make a lousy drug dealer." Derek thumped the book. "Better learn this stuff." He started to turn away, then swung around. "If you do start dealing, I'll drop by and arrest you. Ever seen the inside of a prison?"

"I visited my brother once," Tom admitted.

Derek reined in a sarcastic remark about the sibling, since that would only put Tom on the defensive. "He loves it there, does he?"

"Well, no."

"And you're planning to follow his example for what brilliant reason?" Enough said, he hoped. "Give school your best shot. Sitting in class may feel like prison now, but believe me, it's nothing like it."

Derek set off toward the stage, where Yolanda was conferring with a couple of people. En route, he scanned the room.

Elise, reviewing a paper with a girl, cast uneasy glances toward the table where Vince sat reading aloud to a couple of youngsters. In his present toned condition, Borrego bore only a vague resemblance to the heavy-drinking, heavy-smoking, overweight chief under whom Derek had once served. In his late fifties, the guy had at least changed for the better physically.

Since he'd moved back to Villazon after a brief stint as a private investigator in Santa Ana, though, trouble had followed. First, there'd been a run-in with a prison escapee who claimed he'd been railroaded. In a confrontation at Vince's daughter's house, the ex-chief had shot the man to death.

A few months later, fire had gutted Ben Lyons's apartment in the building where both he and Vince lived. And Norm Kinsey, one of Vince's disgraced former cohorts, had returned seeking revenge against those who'd testified at his dismissal hearing. He'd been foiled by Hale's determination and by his own ailing heart.

Too many incidents to be mere chance, in Derek's opinion. The more he thought about it—especially since his conversation with Marta—the more he believed the source might be one of several officers still loyal to Vince. They were distributed among the bureaus, which would explain how they appeared to have access to a range of information.

He respected Marta's discomfort at spying on her friends. Therefore, the simplest way to check up on Vince appeared to be for Derek himself to volunteer at Villa Corazon. And if working here provided more time with Marta, well, he wouldn't mind. Their chats at the hospital seemed frustratingly brief.

He would have liked to stop and say hello now, but her small charge clearly occupied her full attention. Instead, Derek approached Yolanda and explained that he wished to tutor.

"Great idea. The children, especially the boys who don't have fathers, respond well to men," she told him.

"How should I proceed?" He'd heard that the center required training, which made sense.

"Follow me." Yolanda escorted him to the reception area to fill out forms. "We require a background check, but I don't imagine that'll be a problem in your case. And by the way, I can't thank you enough for participating in the auction."

"My pleasure." No exaggeration there.

He attacked the forms despite the distracting sound of hammering from the playroom. Yolanda, perpetually in demand to answer questions or solve problems, vanished back into the auditorium.

After completing the paperwork, Derek was debating whether to wait around for Marta when he heard low, urgent voices. A man and a woman entered the office area.

He instantly recognized Elise Masterson and Vince Borrego. She sounded angry, he defensive.

"I work during the week. This is the only time I can volunteer," the ex-chief said. "Don't you think the end justifies the inconvenience?"

"Go bestow your good deeds somewhere else. There are lots of other volunteer organizations in Villazon," she snapped.

Don't let him leave Villa Corazon yet. Not till I nail his butt to the wall, Derek thought.

Ben Lyons, brown hair falling into his eyes, poked his head out of the playroom, where he'd been doing repairs. "He's welcome here. Mrs. Rios says so. Don't you agree, Sergeant Reed?"

Put on the spot, Derek muttered, "Far be it from me to argue with Mrs. Rios."

That drew three stares, Ben's puzzled, Vince's skeptical and Elise's surprised. "You're tutoring?" she asked.

"I had so much fun on the stage, I decided to stick around," he joked.

"These kids could use more male role models." Vince stared at Elise. "That wasn't meant as a sexist remark, if anyone's keeping score."

"Oh, blow it out your ear." Pulling on her motorcycle jacket, Elise stomped out to the parking lot.

Ben adjusted his grip on the hammer. "She's got no business holding a grudge. Whatever happened, it was years ago."

To Derek's astonishment, Vince answered, "She has a right to resent me. I acted like a jerk."

The guy seemed sincere. Although Derek didn't trust his former boss, he understood why Yolanda might.

"People should forgive and forget," the nineteen-year-old countered.

"Like you've forgiven your father for being so rigid when you were younger?" Vince prodded.

"That's different!" Clearly unwilling to continue the discussion, Ben disappeared into the playroom.

Vince regarded Derek with a glint of humor. "Touchy subject."

"Guess so." Despite the ex-chief's congenial matter, Derek wasn't ready to unbend. There remained that not-so-minor matter of the department's continuing problem with press leaks.

Yolanda's return short-circuited further comments. "Well, Sergeant, let's schedule your orientation. We're open next Saturday despite the Thanksgiving holiday. Will you be around or are you tied up all weekend?"

"I'm not big on celebrating holidays. Next Saturday would be fine." Derek returned Vince's polite farewell nod, glad to see the man go. Yolanda gave a little wave as well.

"By the way, I like the way you dealt with Tom Bernardi." She must be referring to the rebellious math hater. "He idolizes his older half brother, Billy, who sets a terrible example. Now that he's in jail, Tom's two younger siblings look to *Tom*, since there's no father in the home. Their mother rents my fourth unit, so I've come to know them all fairly well. That's how I was able to persuade Tom to join us."

"What's she like? The mother, I mean." If she had serious problems, as well, that would hurt the boy's chances of going straight.

"She does her best, but she works long hours," Yolanda said. "If you can bring Tom around, you'd be helping the whole family."

"You're suggesting I replace his tutor?" The notion appealed to Derek. He could relate to a kid that age more easily than to, say, a kindergartner.

"She's in over her head. I think I'll pair her with a little girl," the director said. "That is, if you feel comfortable teaching math."

It had been one of Derek's best subjects. His parents had urged him to pursue the field, perhaps to specialize in financial law or become a forensic accountant. He'd loathed the idea of being chained to a desk, but tutoring was a different matter. "I'd enjoy it."

He hadn't expected to feel this way. To him, volunteering had been merely a means to an end. But meeting Tom had put a different spin on things.

Yolanda nodded in confirmation. "By the way, about the holiday—if you're not already booked, I'm hosting a potluck Thanksgiving dinner at my house. We'd love to have you."

He'd declined an invitation to join his parents and siblings on a ski trip, which in his present condition was out of the question. Of course, he still hadn't told the other Reeds about that.

Nevertheless, acting sociable with a bunch of casual acquaintances wasn't Derek's idea of a good time, either. He'd better claim he had plans, even if those plans consisted of eating a frozen turkey dinner and watching a couple of DVDs.

"Well, that's very kind—" He broke off as Marta approached, a wayward strand of hair sticking from the bun atop her head. Without thinking, Derek reached over and tucked it into place.

Marta gave him a small, pleased grin. Their contact had the easy familiarity of lovers, Derek realized.

Yolanda clearly didn't miss the interchange. Smoothly, she said, "Marta's cohosting the event. You'll recognize a lot of the guests. Connie and Hale Crandall, for example."

"You're coming to our annual Thanksgiving party?" Marta beamed. "Wait'll you taste the fabulous food! We all prepare our favorite dishes."

Derek didn't have the heart to refuse. In truth, he no longer wished to. "What can I bring?"

"Do you have a specialty?" Yolanda asked.

"Middle Eastern food." Marta shifted a book bag on her shoulder. "Just kidding."

Derek rather liked the idea. "I'll pick up some hummus and pita if you don't mind eating that on turkey day."

"That suits me fine. We always have Mexican dishes and occasionally Vietnamese," the director said. "I'll see you both there, then."

After she left, Derek noticed how invitingly Marta's jeans and velour top emphasized her figure. He felt a profound urge to kiss the curve of her neck. If she felt the same cravings, they were crazy to deny themselves a return match.

"Shall I pick you up for Thanksgiving?" he suggested as an opening.

Her answer startled him. "I don't think so."

"Why not?"

"Well…a couple of reasons." She hesitated.

When the pause lengthened, he pressed the point. "Have I offended you?"

"Not exactly."

Perhaps his presence here wasn't entirely welcome. "Care to explain?"

"Why are you volunteering at the center?" Marta demanded. "You never mentioned wanting to tutor."

Derek remembered her objection to spying on her friends. Fair enough, but her personal qualms didn't preclude him from snooping on his own.

As he weighed his response, he realized this conversation was too touchy to conduct in the reception area, with volunteers signing in and students passing by. "Mind if we talk outside?"

"Good idea."

The parking lot proved busy as well, so they strolled across the street to the high school. About a dozen cars dotted the blacktop and occasional shouts from behind the low buildings signaled that practices were under way on the athletic fields. Otherwise, the parklike campus appeared deserted.

Derek didn't relish detailing his frame of mind. But he'd rather be frank with Marta than antagonize her.

SHE COULDN'T IMAGINE where she'd found the nerve to question Derek's motives, or the strength to risk angering him. Still, Marta refused to act like a wimp on issues of principle.

She wasn't sure why the matter bothered her so much. The center *did* need more tutors, and once he committed, Derek seemed like the type of person to continue at least until the end of the school year. But the presence of a man with an agenda, even a dear friend, troubled her. She'd helped establish the center as place of refuge and encouragement, not a hunting ground.

Still, what if Vince *had* joined in order to stir up trouble with Elise? He might be the one misusing the center, not Derek.

They navigated a grassy area dappled by sunlight through scattered trees. Memories flowed of her adolescent years— sitting on a low wall eating lunch with Connie, joking with Rachel between classes, holding hands with her boyfriend Joey as they discussed plans for the prom.

When they reached the iron fence surrounding the interior courtyard, they discovered it was unlocked. Clubs might be meeting on a Saturday, or possibly the custodian had opened it to accommodate the athletes. Although she felt like an intruder, Marta escorted Derek to one of the picnic tables in the outdoor lunch area.

"Not exactly luxury accommodations." She sank onto the bench. "I never used to notice how hard these were." She'd been younger and more flexible in those days. And hadn't suffered through a near-fatal car crash, either.

"You attended school here?" Derek took in a poster advertising a drama club production of *Noises Off* and another urging students to place early orders for yearbooks.

"Yes. Where did you graduate from?"

"Estancia." It lay in Costa Mesa, about thirty miles away.

"I'll bet the girls followed you around." She wouldn't blame them.

He shifted sideways, trying to get comfortable on the bench across from her. "I'm sure their parents warned them to give me a wide berth. But yeah, I dated a few girls." He left it at that; no specifics. "So you're afraid I'm faking an interest in tutoring?"

"It's partly my fault," she conceded. "I did tell you about Vince joining the center. But I didn't expect you to dive in without warning. Then today you turn up and *wham!* you're twisting Yolanda around your finger."

"Nobody puts anything over on that lady." His mouth quirked at the notion. "Did I come here to keep an eye on Vince? Sure. But I'm getting kind of excited about teaching. The boy I'll be working with reminds me of myself at that age."

Overhead, a seagull circled and mewed. It had strayed a good twenty miles from the ocean, but those powerful wings could easily return it to the sea.

Marta decided to give Derek the benefit of the doubt. Besides, his comment piqued her interest. "How does he resemble you?"

"He pretends a toughness he doesn't feel. And there's an undercurrent of anger. I'm looking forward to helping channel it."

"Good for you." She sensed he was still holding back. "Derek, why's it so important to you to find out who's tipping off Tracy? I understand that you have a duty, but you're spending your free time on the search. You even tried to enlist me. This seems personal."

Derek's gaze followed the seagull wheeling through the sky. "It is."

"Why?"

He swallowed before continuing. "Between you and me, I don't feel like I'm contributing enough to the police department."

"Everyone says you're doing a great job." The previous community relations officer, according to Rachel, had been ineffective with the press and disorganized in running programs. His departure to accept a private security post had bothered no one.

"I appreciate that, but I can't sit on the sidelines while a traitor undermines the entire force. I didn't choose police work because I enjoy playing footsy with the media. Especially not when there's more at stake." Derek's tone verged on a snarl. "If I have to handle this damn job, I'm going to make the most of it."

Until now, Marta had assumed that his occasional grumbling stemmed from a desire to downplay what amounted to a promotion. An open display of ambition within the department could alienate friends. But his anger made that motive seem unlikely.

"You didn't request a transfer?" she asked.

"It wasn't my choice, believe me."

"If you feel that way, why did you accept the position?" she asked.

He responded grimly. "Sometimes you have to accept what your superiors think is best."

Considering the high visibility of the post, Marta didn't believe he'd been assigned as a form of punishment. "Surely the chief would send you back to the detective squad if you told him how you feel."

"Things don't work that way. Too complicated." His tone indicated he didn't wish to discuss the subject further.

Marta respected his privacy. And though she still didn't support the idea of Derek's joining the center as a sort of mole, he obviously *had* taken an interest in a boy who'd been driving his tutor crazy. "So you think you can knock that chip off Tom's shoulder?"

The change of subject eased the tension in his bearing. "The kid needs to understand how the real world operates and why he should grab his chance at an education. I expect this will be a learning experience for both of us."

"You don't have much experience with children?" He'd mentioned two younger siblings.

"Not really." He didn't elaborate, but at least he'd stopped scowling.

For no reason other than simple curiosity, Marta asked, "Want a few of your own?"

An expression of something akin to regret vanished quickly. "Once, I'd have said yes, but the older I get, the less I consider myself the family type. My big holiday plans consisted of figuring out which brand of frozen turkey dinner to buy, and that was fine with me. If Yolanda hadn't invited me, I'd have been the biggest recluse in town on Thursday."

"You've got friends," she pointed out. "You don't have to be alone."

He stared blankly past her. "I'm happier by myself. Most of the time."

"You didn't sound happy when you said that." Marta reached out to touch Derek's hand. She was half-afraid he'd draw away, but instead he enfolded her hand in his. "I hate spending holidays alone," she continued. "Being around friends is like—" she searched for a comparison "—like luxuriating in a hot tub on a cold night."

He chuckled. "I can relate to that." More seriously: "You're naturally congenial. It's a gift, and other people appreciate you. Frankly, I might not have accepted Yolanda's offer if you hadn't been going."

The revelation pleased her. Still, she added honestly, "People enjoy your company, too. You shouldn't shut them out."

He brought her palm to his lips, tracing a tantalizing trail across the sensitive skin and reminding her of that night in the spa. "Does that include you?"

"Of course!" She'd thought the importance she placed on their friendship must be obvious.

"I'm not the one who slammed the door, so to speak," he said.

"You're twisting my words. Unfair!" Marta laughed a little breathlessly, nearly losing her train of thought as his dark eyes fixed on her.

"Perhaps what happened between us didn't affect you, but I feel like we left something unfinished," Derek said.

Did he really? Her chest squeezed. But his phrasing reminded her that "finishing" their affair meant exactly that. "Our night together meant a lot to me. You're a special guy, Derek."

"Then why do you keep backing off?" he pressed. "Why not enjoy this as long as it lasts?"

Marta couldn't continue to dance around the truth. "Because I know what you're like!" she burst out. "Sergeant Hit-and-Run!"

Understanding glimmered. "And you aren't willing to be left."

He was probing too close to her vulnerabilities. "I refuse to ruin what we've got."

"Which is?"

"Talking. Kidding. Bucking each other up," she summarized. "Having fun."

"How much fun can we have in the lobby of the Mesa View Medical Center?" Derek returned.

"That depends on who's watching!" Embarrassed, she wiggled her hand free on the pretext of replacing a bobby pin in her hair. "By the way, Russ saw us practically kissing. He's not blind."

Beneath Derek's grin, she thought she detected real fondness. Or perhaps her fantasies were running away with her. "I'm not ashamed of what happened," he said.

"Neither am I. But don't go telling anyone." Her cheeks heated. "I like privacy as much as you do."

"Great." Derek stretched. "Now that we're in agreement, why don't I pick you up on Thanksgiving like I suggested."

Marta longed to be Derek's date again, even on a casual basis. However, she couldn't accept. "I promised to help Yolanda prepare. I'll be arriving early."

He released a disappointed breath, or perhaps she only imagined that. Still, she *had* been rather hard on him today.

"We'll both be teaching next Saturday," she ventured. "We could have coffee afterward."

"Or take a dip in a hot tub?" he suggested.

"Coffee." Marta regarded him steadily.

"Okay. For starters." He appeared to be searching for another idea. And found one. "Christmas."

"Sorry?"

"What are you doing for Christmas?" Derek inquired with a mischievous air.

"You can't be asking me for a date on Christmas!"

"Just answer the question."

"I haven't decided." She wondered why he'd raised the subject. "My dad and Bryn celebrate with her sister in San Diego." In the past, she'd joined Connie, but this December would be the Crandalls' and the McKenzies' first season as nuclear families and she hated to intrude.

"How about performing an act of charity? You can run interference between me and my so-called nearest and dearest. Don't bother with presents. I'll buy them in your name." Derek folded his arms.

What an outrageous idea! "You can't invite me home to meet your folks," Marta protested. "They'll assume we're involved, when we're just friends."

"They'll be grateful to have a buffer between them and the Grinch," Derek countered. "As an added lure, my sister has a baby. Don't tell me you wouldn't enjoy sharing Minnie's first Christmas."

The invitation seemed so unlikely that Marta began to fear she'd dreamed this entire episode. Perhaps she'd fallen asleep after her tutoring session. Any minute she'd wake up in

Yolanda's office, slumped over a desk with her head on her arms. However, the air smelled of eucalyptus, and odors never invaded her sleep. "I'll bet she's adorable."

"Done." Pushing away from the bench, Derek rose. She saw something that looked like pain flash across his face.

"Are you getting rheumatism? You aren't *that* old." Marta straightened.

"I'm not over the hill yet." He eased around the table. Transfixed, she found herself unable to stir as his thumb grazed her cheek and he brushed her forehead with a kiss.

In another minute, she'd curve against him. His unexpected behavior left her too entranced to withdraw.

Mercifully, the thumping approach of a custodian's cleaning cart roused her and sent him backward a step. "We'd better scram or the principal might give us detention," Marta said, and limped across the courtyard.

Derek kept pace. "I used to enjoy detention. Dropping my books, throwing spitballs when the monitor wasn't looking and generally creating havoc."

"A paragon of virtue." They crossed the street side by side.

"I never claimed to be virtuous." Low and sensual, his voice tickled her ear. "And there are all kinds of friendships, Marta."

"That's true. For instance, we've got a really weird one." Refusing to give him any further chance to penetrate her defenses, she headed toward her car. "Till Thursday."

"What time's dinner?" he called.

"Three-thirty." Yolanda had chosen that hour to accommodate police officers who had to work the day shift, which ended at three.

"I'll be there." Derek swung into his sedan. Idly, Marta wondered why he'd traded in the sports car that had been the envy of his fellow cops.

The man had a lot of mystifying aspects. On the short drive home, she reviewed them: Derek's admitted dissatisfaction with his job. His invitation to Christmas, which she'd accepted without quite intending to. His desire to see her again outside their established routine.

Was it possible he truly cared for her? That if they proceeded slowly, perhaps he wouldn't bolt?

Marta knew she ought to stop now while her heart remained, if not whole, at least functional. That, however, meant settling for a life of what-ifs. A life of temporary safety with no chance of wild, exhilarating bliss.

She was neither a dimwit nor a coward. She'd have to proceed with caution, she decided.

But proceed she would.

Chapter Ten

A block before he reached Yoland's address in the town's older section, Derek spotted a middle-aged couple on the sidewalk carrying a covered dish. They, too, it appeared, were heading for Yolanda's, and judging by the number of cars parked beneath the palms and jacarandas, most of the other guests had already arrived.

As promised, he recognized many of the guests gathered in front of Yolanda's white-stucco fourplex. Through the windshield, he picked out several coworkers from the PD, a couple of center volunteers and Ben Lyons. No sign of Vince Borrego, who'd probably chosen to spend the occasion with his daughter's family.

Makeshift tables covered with holiday-themed cloths dotted the yard, flanked by a motley assortment of folding chairs. The weather was sunny and crisp, and while many guests wore sweaters or jackets, others sported the shorts and tank tops that typified Southern California attire year-round.

As he cruised past, Derek caught sight of Marta talking to Tracy Johnson. He wished Yolanda hadn't invited the reporter, since her presence meant he needed to guard his tongue. Of course, he'd have to do that anyway.

His annoyance disappeared when he heard Marta laugh aloud at the antics of some children. To Derek, her delight lit up the yard. Inviting her to Christmas had been a terrific idea, he reflected as he hunted for a free spot along the curb. He loathed trying to pretend he felt comfortable with his family as they shared jokes he didn't get and referred to outings in which he hadn't participated.

He'd taken a stab at understanding them when, after his diagnosis, the chief had insisted on a couple of sessions with a psychologist. As the wife of a retired firefighter, Dr. Eugenia Wrigley appreciated the stresses on rescue personnel, and with her help, he'd grasped how young and immature his parents must have been when he was born. Also that compliant children like his brother and sister had been a lot easier to raise than their defiant older brother.

Those perceptions had diluted Derek's anger, although they'd failed to bridge the gap between him and his family. Besides, the sessions had focused primarily on adjusting to Parkinson's and to his reassignment. While Dr. Wrigley had smoothed his transition, she couldn't work miracles.

Derek found a free space around the corner. Other families in the neighborhood must be celebrating as well because, as he walked, he inhaled delicious scents and heard voices drifting from windows. Usually, witnessing the close connections of others left him with a hollow, irritable feeling. Not today. He simply looked forward to sharing the event with Marta.

In a corner yard, a kitten poked its nose out of a bush. Derek broke stride. Ginger-striped and tiny, the animal looked too young to be out on its own. Suddenly, in one sinuous movement, a large gray cat swooped down on the kitten and plucked it up by the neck. Mom to the rescue. No outside assistance required.

He continued around the corner and was almost at the fourplex when he nearly got clobbered in the shins. The perpetrator was a boy of about three, zooming on a tricycle.

"Whoa!" Derek sidestepped barely in time to avoid a collision. He glanced around for a parent or sitter, but no one at the fourplex appeared to be paying heed.

The kid wheeled to the corner, reversed course and began

pedaling back at full speed. Someone might get hurt, either the kid or whoever he slammed into, particularly an elderly person. Derek's illness had increased his awareness of the dangers posed by rambunctious youngsters.

"Slow down!" A couple of fast strides and he caught the boy's handlebars, pacing by the side as the trike eased to a halt. "Where's your mom?"

"At work." The little boy regarded him boldly.

"Who's watching you?"

A girl of about six ran by on the lawn, chasing another girl. "Our brother. Good luck finding him!" Off she went.

"Who're you?" The little boy stared up from the seat.

"Officer Reed." Best to identify himself as an authority figure. This kid didn't seem easily abashed.

"You gonna bust me?" That seemed rather precocious for a preschooler.

"No. Just trying to prevent you from knocking people over," Derek said.

The boy wasn't in danger with so many adults around, although he certainly needed better supervision. About to go in search of Yolanda, Derek saw a skinny, half-grown boy lope toward them.

He and Tom Bernardi recognized each other at almost the same moment. "Oh, hi," the ten-year-old said.

Their mother had left this youngster in charge of a tot? Struggling single mom, oldest son in jail, kids raising kids. He wondered where the father was.

"Hi." Deciding that a lecture was a poor way to start a relationship, Derek stuck to the facts. "This little ruffian nearly bowled me over."

"That's Boris."

"Boris? Unusual name," he observed.

"Yeah, his dad's Russian or something. His and Kaylie's." Tom eyed Derek warily, as if anticipating a snide comment.

Best not to comment at all. Instead, he asked, "What's to eat?"

"There's some chips over there." Tom indicated a side table.

"Great." Derek strode over with the two boys trailing him.

En route, he exchanged greetings with other guests. Marta, however, must have gone inside, and he didn't see Yolanda.

Derek piled chips, cut vegetables and ranch-style dip onto a paper plate. "This is perfect. Thanks for steering me."

Tom passed a couple of chips to his brother. "Mrs. Rios says you're gonna tutor me."

"Okay with you?"

A nod. "So you're a cop?"

Derek conceded the point. "Right now I work in community relations. Visit schools, coordinate programs and try to keep people safe."

Boris peered through a fringe of blond hair. "You got a gun?"

"Yes." Despite the peaceful nature of his position, Derek was required to carry a firearm.

"Can I see it?" Tom asked eagerly.

Derek didn't consider a weapon to be a curiosity piece. "Not right now. If your mom approves, one day I'll take you to a shooting range." Knowledge of gun safety encouraged respect for arms, in his opinion.

"Cool!" Tom declared.

Much as he appreciated getting acquainted with his student, Derek had run out of topics. He wished Marta would come outside. Judging by the aroma wafting through the window, someone, maybe Marta, had removed corn bread from the oven. "Is your mom going to miss dinner?"

"She should be here soon." Tom frowned. "She promised."

On tiptoe, Boris groped into the chip bowl. Then, clutching a handful of chips, the smaller boy trotted toward Ben Lyons, who'd been pressed into service setting up folding chairs. "See you later," Tom called, and followed.

The two boys seemed drawn to any older male in the vicinity, Derek reflected. He understood Yolanda's eagerness to assign Tom a male tutor.

A voice nearby deflected his attention to Frank Ferguson, who was helping himself to cheese puffs. "Good to see you here, Derek."

"Thanks. You too."

The detective captain's single status probably explained his participating in a potluck Thanksgiving meal. "Congratulations on joining the center," he said. "That should be good for the department's image."

"I hope so." Although he'd worked closely with Frank in the past, Derek hesitated to reveal his plan to spy on Vince. He didn't anticipate trouble about exceeding his job description, but if his plan bore no results, he preferred to get as little egg on his face as possible.

"You should meet lots of single gals there." Obviously, the captain put his own interpretation on Derek's motives. "Guess you've run through the nurses by now."

Although Derek used to enjoy his playboy image, it had begun to grate in the past year. In fact, since the evening with Marta, Derek felt embarrassed about that pleasure-seeking, insensitive persona—especially since his reputation had discouraged her from continuing their affair.

Still, he'd rather not discuss such a personal topic. "Exactly," he responded.

The last thing he wanted was to let anyone at work suspect that he'd changed. He wanted whatever was developing between him and Marta to remain out of the spotlight.

At last she emerged from the fourplex, carrying a plate piled with corn bread squares. The sun picked out red highlights in the soft brown hair floating around her shoulders.

In an embroidered peasant blouse and a ruffled turquoise skirt, she looked fresh and sweet. Several other guys watched her with interest, Derek noticed, and felt an unfamiliar spurt of possessiveness.

Marta stopped to speak to Ben. As Derek approached, she was explaining that Tom's mother had suffered car trouble at the hospital. "Would you mind going and picking her up, Ben?"

"I'd go, except my car's been acting up, too," the young man said apologetically. "I'm not sure how I'm going to get to classes this week, let alone deliver pizzas."

Frank beat Derek to the punch in offering his services. "I'll fetch the lady if you'll come along to point her out." When Ben hesitated, he added, "And we can talk about borrowing some wheels for you. Your dad drives a staff car most days. I could speak to him about lending you his personal vehicle."

"He'd never do that," Ben scoffed.

"You should give your father more credit."

Ben frowned. "Well, I sure could use a car." As Frank shepherded the young man away, Derek appreciated the captain's effort to smooth over the rift between the chief and his son.

"Vince's teaching me how to tune cars," announced Tom, who'd stayed behind. "Maybe he'll fix my mom's for her."

"Think you might be a mechanic someday?" Derek inquired

"Maybe." The boy considered. "Does that involve math?"

"What do you think?"

Tom shrugged. "I guess so."

"You bet it does." Fortunately, the lad didn't request details. Auto repair wasn't one of Derek's skills, although he could have invented some sort of problem involving miles per gallon.

The tinkle of a china bell silenced the chattering in the yard. "Dinner's served!" Yolanda called. "Please form two lines. No shoving, kids! There's plenty to eat."

Tom scooted off with his little brother. Marta accompanied Derek toward one of the lines snaking through the yard.

"You have a knack for getting through to that boy. You're mellowing, Sarge." She brushed his arm, and Derek felt an impulse to touch her in return. Then, catching Connie's speculative gaze on them, he reluctantly put a little space between himself and Marta.

"If I'm less of an ogre, that's your influence." True enough.

Tracy Johnson fell into place behind them in line. Derek addressed the reporter. "Searching for news or simply enjoying the holiday?"

"Like you, I'm never entirely off duty, but I try not to let that cramp my style," she replied. "Say, I missed the details of your auction date. How did it go, you two?"

"We survived," he said dryly.

"And we're still on speaking terms," Marta added.

"Who'd have imagined a bachelor auction could have such romantic results? I hear Andie O'Reilly's gone out three times with her lawyer." Tracy obviously kept her ear to the ground. "Maybe I should write a follow-up article."

Derek hoped not. "Planning to include yourself?"

The reporter responded with an uncharacteristic blush. "I don't think that's a good idea." Peering past them, she uttered a startled "Speaking of bachelors!"

Joel marched into the yard, one hand shading his eyes as he scanned the crowd. He must have just finished watch-commander duty.

"His family lives around here. Why isn't he with them?" Marta mused aloud.

Tracy vibrated in place and finally, as if unable to contain herself, waved. With a grin, Joel loped toward her.

Well, well, Derek thought. For all his protestations, the guy had obviously forgiven Tracy for that article. The basketball tickets hadn't hurt, but they didn't account for the fond look on the guy's face.

Joel slowed, sobering as he acknowledged Derek and Marta's presence. "Oh, hey. I was driving by and smelled food. Mind if I join you?"

"If the people behind us don't object." Marta soon received good-natured permission.

"What brings you here?" Joel asked Tracy, although Derek strongly suspected this meeting had been prearranged.

Her features relaxed into a smile. "Gee, I'm not sure."

."Nowhere else to go?" he teased.

"Too many enemies." She pretended to agree.

"You haven't ticked off anybody here?" He folded his arms.

"I've ticked off practically *everyone* here. Maybe I should hire a bodyguard." She widened her eyes. "Know anyone with that kind of training?"

"You mean a Rambo who hunts helpless little animals?"

"Precisely."

Derek and Marta exchanged amused glances at the discovery that this pair had managed to turn their earlier conflict into a source of humor. Amazing that they'd rebounded from a falling-out that would have doomed most relationships.

Around the yard, he noted the good spirits that prevailed as the guests piled their plates or waited patiently. Connie and Hale were serving Skip, a teenage boy and girl stole kisses whenever their parents didn't appear to be watching, and Yolanda observed the whole setting with an air of satisfaction.

The strangest feeling crept over Derek as he listened to the banter between his pal and the reporter and as the breeze persuaded Marta to shift into the shelter of his larger body. A sense that he belonged here with these people. He suspended all worries about his illness, about the future and about his ability to strike a balance between his moodiness and his desire to be with Marta.

For once, Derek simply allowed himself to be happy.

IF MARTA HAD HER WAY, a fairy godmother would whisk her and Derek to a desert island. Although she cherished her friends and acquaintances, did they *have* to keep interrupting?

No sooner had the two of them sat at a table with Joel and Tracy than Connie's mother arrived. She cooed over Marta's Mexican peasant skirt and blouse while sizing up Derek.

Looking much younger than her fifty-seven years, the wealthy divorcée exuded glamour. Marta thanked her aunt again for the makeover and new dress, and introduced the man who'd been the object.

"Money well spent, obviously," Anna responded. "So, are you young folks an item now?"

Marta nearly choked on a bite of sweet potato. Thank goodness Skip chose that moment to accost his grandmother. "Gramma Anna! Mom says I can have pie if you help me cut it."

Silently, Marta blessed her cousin, whom she was certain had engineered Skip's interruption. "Sorry about that," she told Derek when Skip had tugged Anna out of earshot.

"Hey, I'm flattered." Usually he tensed when anyone fussed over him, but the food must have tempered his spirits.

Marta took another bite of her own food, the portions of which she'd made smaller than usual. Ironically, a full stomach seemed to soothe the indigestion that had bothered her for the past few weeks, as a result of which she'd overindulged in her favorite comfort foods and put on a couple of extra pounds.

She'd finished her turkey, stuffing, mashed potatoes and green beans by the time Ben and Frank arrived with Nina Bernardi. The nurse, whose deeply lined skin reflected her heavy smoking, hugged her younger children and thanked Tom for watching them.

The boy drew himself up straight and glanced at Derek as if hoping he'd heard. Derek smiled in approval, and, pleased, Tom hurried to fix iced tea for his mother. He seemed eager to show how helpful he could be.

"Like I said, you've sure gotten through to Tom." Marta smiled. "Having you as a mentor could make a huge difference to him."

She'd never met Tom's dad or the subsequent boyfriend who'd fathered Kaylie and Boris. In fact, she'd first met the boy a mere six weeks ago, after his mother rented the remodeled apartment. The first day Yolanda brought him to the tutoring center, his hunched shoulders and averted gaze had testified to his low self-esteem.

"Still see parallels to yourself?" Marta asked.

"He's more open about his needs than I used to be," Derek admitted. "I never let anyone see my vulnerabilities."

"Even now?"

"Confessions aren't my style." He regarded his nearly empty plate. "I'm ready for seconds. Can I fetch you anything?"

Marta's stomach had resumed churning. She decided to withdraw and take an antacid. "No, thanks. I'd better pop into the kitchen. I'm not sure if I remembered to switch off the oven."

"You're going in? You'd better not start cleaning up, not after all the work you've done already," Tracy objected.

"There's a designated crew, and I'm pleased to say I'm not on it. I'll see you in a couple of minutes." She hurried off, unsure why she didn't simply tell them about her indigestion.

Perhaps because that didn't seem polite. And because Derek wasn't the only person who preferred not to wear his weaknesses on his sleeve.

Marta navigated between crowded tables. While a number of children had resumed playing on the sidewalk, the adults lingered over their meals. Double and triple helpings of dessert appeared the norm, a tribute to the bountiful offerings of pies, cakes, brownies and cookies.

Memories of past Thanksgivings drifted into her thoughts. During Marta's childhood, her mother, Vivian, used to invite large groups for the holiday. Connie's family had been among the regulars before her parents divorced. As for Marta's dad, Harry Lawson had appreciated the dishes, but as an insurance executive, he felt more at ease with facts and figures than among people.

The Thanksgiving after Vivian's death, the two of them had dined with Connie's father, Jim—Harry's brother—and his second wife, Mila. Since Connie spent the holiday with Anna, the only other person present had been Jim and Mila's oldest son, Cole, then a chunky toddler. To Marta, the meal had seemed cold and silent, enlivened only when Cole upchucked most of his dinner.

If she weren't careful, she might lose some of hers, she realized when she reached the kitchen. Turkey carcasses lay on cutting boards, flanked by other remnants of meal preparation: a bowl rimmed with bits of stuffing, beaters encrusted with mashed potato and a pot in which leftover gravy congealed.

Marta's innards rebelled. The sight of Yolanda entering with an almost empty bowl of brussels sprouts proved to be the last straw. Unable to stammer an excuse, she plunged through an inner doorway and beelined for the bathroom.

How humiliating. She hadn't lost a meal since a bout with flu years earlier.

After throwing up, Marta rinsed her mouth. She scrabbled inside her purse for the roll of antacids she'd begun carrying.

A slice of pumpkin pie ought to settle the sourness, she reflected as she emerged. To her surprise, Yolanda stood waiting in the hall.

"We'd better talk." The older woman watched her worriedly.

Marta's throat constricted. "What's wrong?"

"Let's go find some privacy."

Marta trailed the older woman into a bedroom-turned-den. Yolanda gestured her to a love seat. "I'm aware that this qualifies as none of my business, but since you don't have a mother and your two closest friends are busy with their new marriages, I'm appointing myself your confidante."

"About what?" Subliminally, though, Marta already suspected the answer. And dreaded facing it.

"I'm not sitting in judgment on whatever happened between you and Sergeant Reed last month." Yolanda brushed a shock of white-laced black hair from her forehead. "By the way, if you two behaved like a pair of saints, I'm completely off track and I apologize."

Marta laced her fingers in her lap. She couldn't be

pregnant. Not when she was finally getting her education on track after a decade-long interruption. And not by Derek who, despite his recent affability, remained the most unlikely husband prospect she knew.

"We used precautions," she mumbled at last, aware that wasn't entirely true.

"The only one hundred percent precaution is abstinence." Yolanda sounded like a sex-education video. "Let's get practical. How late is your period?"

"My periods aren't regular." The accident, surgeries and medications had wreaked havoc with Marta's hormones. "I was afraid I might not be fertile."

Yolanda leaned forward from her armchair. "Would giving birth put you in danger? Because of your injuries, I mean."

"No. Thank goodness." Marta's voice broke. She hated the hot surge of tears that slid down her cheeks.

"Have you taken a pregnancy test?" Yolanda asked gently. "No."

"That's your first step." A sigh. "If it's positive, what will you do?"

"I couldn't…" Couldn't tell Derek? She'd begin to show soon enough, and she'd already informed him that he was the first guy she'd slept with in more than ten years. Besides, Marta refused to deceive him about such an important matter. "I don't know."

"We'll get through this." Yolanda's reassuring voice reminded her of Vivian. If only her mom were here—a thought that spurred more tears. "Lots of families are desperate to adopt, if you choose that route."

"I—" Marta broke off. No sense putting the cart before the horse, as Mom used to say. "Do you suppose there's a drugstore open on Thanksgiving?"

"I'm sure there is." The older woman waited sympathetically.

"I'll say goodbye to my friends." Yet Marta didn't dare go outside with tearstains on her cheeks. Even if she managed to scrub away the worst of the evidence, her distress would be obvious. "No. I can't face them. I parked in back. Will you forgive me if I sneak out?"

"Of course. I'll make some excuse. There's the ever-popular crashing headache," her hostess suggested. "For credibility, it beats an abduction by space aliens."

"Thanks." Marta smiled wanly and collected her purse. "I've always been able to talk to my friends, but right now I don't feel like confiding in anyone except you."

"I'm honored." Yolanda accompanied her to the rear door. Her final advice was: "Don't wait too long to level with the guy. I suspect your sergeant has more depth than you give him credit for."

Maybe too much depth, Marta thought as she fled to her car. Too many layers of repressed emotion.

If this proved to be a false alarm, she'd learned her lesson, she resolved. No more tempting fate. Despite her craving for Derek's arms, she would summon the strength to control herself in future.

She drove to an open drugstore and bought a kit. Took it home and shakily followed the directions. The stick emerged bright pink.

Pregnant. The test was more than ninety-nine percent accurate, according to the box.

Marta strained to accept that a tiny little person, part her and part Derek, had begun to grow. That had to be a miracle. If only the circumstances weren't so overwhelming.

She huddled on the couch, hugging a well-worn bear that Rachel had given her years ago, and tried to sort out her feelings. Even her most optimistic visions didn't present Derek as a doting dad. Furthermore, the situation risked humiliating him publicly. There'd be jokes about Sergeant Can't-Keep-His-Pants-On and, given his position, embarrassment for the department.

He would probably offer child support, possibly promise

to stand by her. But emotionally, just when she'd hoped he might risk caring, this was likely to drive him back behind his protective mask.

Thanks to a bit of poor judgment and worse timing, Marta was going to lose the man she loved before she ever really had him.

Chapter Eleven

Who'd have figured there was so much to learn about teaching?

Derek had arrived early at Villa Corazon on Saturday afternoon, hoping to catch Marta before she began her tutoring session, but no sooner had he signed in than Yolanda whisked him through the reception area and auditorium to an area set aside on the stage. Here, she introduced him to Ginger Lindeman, a high-school teacher who trained volunteers.

Of course, Derek had expected to review Tom's level of mathematics. He hadn't realized, however, that he would have to absorb information about educational strategies. Students, it seemed, displayed a variety of different learning styles. In addition, many youngsters harbored a fear of math, which created the need to establish a constructive psychological atmosphere. Fortunately, he'd already achieved that by following his instincts, Ginger said when he related his discussions with the boy.

The fun part came when Derek got to play a couple of math-oriented games on a laptop, a gift to the center from a local corporation. Tom's current tutor reserved such games as a reward, according to Ginger. She agreed, however, when Derek proposed using them more extensively to help the boy understand concepts and to make the subject enjoyable.

At the end of two hours, Ginger signaled that they were

done for the day. "We've covered the basics. Another session to review the math and go over what we studied today, and you'll be ready for one-on-one tutoring."

Derek would have preferred to plow ahead, even though his brain felt waterlogged. Still, he hated to waste another week. "Are you available one evening after work? I'd like to start with Tom next Saturday."

"I'll be happy to arrange it." Thoughtfully, Ginger added, "I'm pleasantly surprised that you're doing this. Dad always described you as a playboy." Her father, Justin Lindeman, was the traffic lieutenant.

"And I always described him as a crusty old bast…codger," Derek returned jovially. He liked Justin, a longtime Vince loyalist who'd warmed to Will's leadership in recent months.

"You seem sincerely drawn to teaching," Ginger went on. "From what Yolanda told me, you have a knack for appealing to the child on his level without condescending."

"I don't believe in talking down to people," Derek agreed.

"Igniting that spark is an art." She closed her notebook. "Don't sell yourself short."

Even as he thanked her, he didn't completely believe the compliment. Hitting the right note with Tom had been more luck than talent.

After helping clear the materials away, Derek gazed over an auditorium full of students and tutors. Marta, who must have entered during his time with Ginger, flashed him a smile and settled at a desk with a student.

Her abrupt departure on Thursday still disturbed him. A sudden headache might signal serious trouble, although she looked all right today. Since the shock of discovering he had Parkinson's, Derek had become less willing to dismiss other people's symptoms as minor.

He'd considered phoning her later to see how she was. However, he hadn't wanted to risk waking her in case she'd dropped off to sleep. Instead, he'd stopped by the hospital yesterday at midmorning, to find her on duty but lacking her usual sparkle.

"It's just a bug," she'd said wearily. "I've got a doctor's appointment this afternoon, but I think I'm nearly over it."

He tried not to worry. Still, the sight of her healthy glow now came as a relief.

Derek hoped she'd be able to go out with him after her teaching session, as they'd discussed last week. Thursday's abrupt end to their meal had left him feeling shortchanged.

Sore after sitting for hours, he descended from the stage. The course to the exit took him past the table where Tom's frustrated tutor labored to engage the squirming boy's interest. "Hey," Derek called. "How's it going?"

"How do you think?" Tom snapped.

Startled by the sharp response, Derek paused. "What's eating you?"

Anger crackled in the boy's voice. "*You* were supposed to tutor me."

Apparently no one had explained about the delay. "I am. Next Saturday. I had my first training session today and I'm coming back later this week to finish getting ready."

Out of the boy's line of sight, the tutor's mouth formed the words *Thank you.*"

Tom shoved overlong bangs off his forehead. "You have to *learn* how to teach?"

"That's right." Ignoring a pang in his hip, Derek picked up a math book from where it had fallen on the floor and placed it on the desk.

"Didn't you already go to college?"

He supposed that at Tom's age he, too, had assumed graduates must know everything. "Sure, but acquiring advanced skills requires further study. For instance, to become an officer, I studied police science."

Tom brightened. "What exactly did you learn?"

"How to collar crooks without getting killed. When to

shoot and when not to. Interviewing a suspect. High-speed driving. And a lot more."

The boy seemed fascinated. "That sounds like fun."

"I'm interrupting your session." Derek clapped him on the shoulder. "You've got a few minutes left. Put them to good use."

"Okay." Reluctantly, the boy returned to his worksheet.

When Derek sneaked another glance at Marta, he caught a glint of approval. Although she appeared absorbed in helping her student read, she'd obviously been observing.

A short while later, a bell marked the end of the hour. Derek angled between tables to reach her and waited until her student departed. Then he raised the subject uppermost in his mind. "How're you feeling?"

Marta capped her pen. "Better."

"The doctor didn't diagnose anything serious?"

"No." She tucked the pen and a notebook into her purse.

She didn't normally act so reticent. "Was it a migraine?" Derek prodded.

"Not exactly."

Something seemed amiss. "We don't need to discuss it here. I'm taking you out, remember?"

Marta's dubious expression dampened his spirits. "I'm not sure I'm up to going anywhere. Besides," she added, "Elise and I promised Yolanda we'd sort through a pile of donated textbooks."

If she truly felt okay, her obligation posed only a temporary impediment. "No problem. I'll return in an hour and we'll get a cup of coffee. Okay?"

She wrinkled her nose. "Not coffee."

"Herbal tea?" Hearing no objection, Derek concluded, "Done."

"You're irrepressible."

"At the very least."

He headed out of the auditorium. A couple of turns around the block ought to stretch his muscles and settle his mood.

Most likely, Marta's reluctance stemmed from the hesitation she'd expressed previously about him, Derek supposed. He didn't understand why sharing refreshments and a conversation should be threatening, though.

As he passed through the office wing, the sound of hammering drew his gaze to the playroom. Ben, sweat darkening his T-shirt, was installing cubbyholes along one wall.

The cabinetry appeared well crafted. Will would be proud of his son if he knew, which he probably didn't.

Outside, beneath an overcast sky, Derek spotted a dark blue late-model sedan wedged between a red compact and a dented van. The chief's car. It must be on loan to Ben—who, with youthful carelessness, had left a window lowered.

Derek didn't intend to nag the kid about respecting his father's property. In any case, he hoped the loan marked the start of a more positive phase in the father and son's relationship.

MARTA TRIED to think of an excuse to cancel the date. She wasn't prepared to talk to Derek.

After half an hour of sorting, she lost her focus and sat staring blankly at the books spread on the storeroom table. Elise, who'd been muttering angrily since spotting Vince a few minutes earlier, took no notice.

Yesterday's appointment with the obstetrician, Dr. LaShandra Bennett, had confirmed Marta's pregnancy. "You're large for six weeks," the physician had commented, using the date of Marta's last menstrual cycle to mark the start of the pregnancy. "Otherwise, you're fine. I'll schedule an ultrasound to rule out any complications, especially considering your prior trauma."

"You think something's wrong?" Marta had asked anxiously.

"No. I just prefer to err on the side of caution."

Dr. Bennett, who often bought breath mints at the gift shop, was aware of Marta's unwed status. "Regardless of circumstances, a baby is a blessing," the older woman had said gently. "You should feel good about this."

"Before or after I upchuck?" Marta had attempted to joke.

"Eat lots of small meals and the nausea should pass by the second trimester." The doctor produced a prenatal packet that included sample vitamins. "How's the father taking this?"

"He doesn't know."

"Are you in a serious relationship?"

Marta's shoulders sagged. "We're friends. And maybe not even that once he hears this news."

"He does have legal obligations," the doctor pointed out.

"I suppose." Marta couldn't think that far ahead.

She had dressed in a daze. So many details to take care of before her mid-July due date, from scheduling the ultrasound to registering for childbirth classes. Above all, the necessity of deciding what to do about the baby. And how to tell Derek.

A baby! Impossible to deny the truth any longer. How could she relinquish a child who seemed like such a miracle? Yet even if she decided on adoption, she'd still have to inform Derek.

"I can't." Marta didn't realize she'd spoken aloud until Elise stopped thumping books around.

"Can't what?"

"Go out with Derek again," Marta blurted. "He asked me to go have coffee after we finish."

"Why not?" The policewoman wiped a smudge from her rose-colored blouse. She'd begun wearing more feminine clothes now that she was dating Mike.

"Because…" For now, Marta had decided to keep her condition secret even from her friends. Instead, she said, "Because if the gorgeous women he dates can't hold on to Sergeant Hit-and-Run, what chance do I have?"

"He invited *you*, not them." Elise eyed her sympathetically. "You're scared, that's all. Remember—nothing ventured, noth-ing gained."

As if I haven't gained too much already! "Maybe I'll re-schedule."

"Mike says putting off our problems makes us obsess about

them." Elise flipped through a damaged textbook and set it on the reject pile. "He's right. We can't control what other people do, only how we respond to them."

Sage advice, except considering the source. "How about you?"

Elise's forehead puckered. "What about me?"

"You're still stewing over Chief Borrego," Marta noted. "Did you ever confront him about the problems he caused you?"

The patrolwoman folded her arms. "I filed a grievance, testified and forced him to retire. That ought to be enough."

"Apparently not. You turn purple when anyone mentions his name, and you're in a huff about his volunteering."

"So?"

"So quit fuming and deal with the situation." Usually Marta offered compassion rather than tough advice. The change in hormones must be affecting her mood, she reflected.

"Vince hasn't apologized," Elise replied truculently. "He thinks I ought to forget the whole thing. Well, I shouldn't have to."

"Tell him," Marta urged.

"I'm afraid I'll punch the creep!"

"No, you won't. Lay it on the line and he either apologizes or demonstrates that he's still a louse." Since that didn't seem an adequate outcome, Marta proposed, "If he doesn't give a reasonable response, discuss your issues with Yolanda. That might change her belief that he's reformed."

Elise's mouth pursed. "Tell you what. I'll confront Vince if you'll meet Derek for coffee."

Unfair! "What's that got to do with anything?"

"If I can tackle my issues, so can you." Elise tossed another book on the reject pile. "Well? Yes or no?"

Marta really wished her friend would resolve this business with Vince. As for Derek, he had to be told the truth sooner or later.

"Yes," she said.

Her friend returned to sorting books. As for Marta, doubts assailed her immediately.

"There he is," Elise hissed.

Marta turned. Through the glass they could see that Vince had stopped across the otherwise empty hall, facing the playroom. His back was to them.

A scowling Elise rose and went out, nearly colliding with Vince, who'd been talking to Ben. "Hold on!" she snapped.

"What can I do for you?" His voice carried clearly to Marta. "And don't keep telling me to volunteer elsewhere. I like working with kids. Sorry if that offends you, but I can't please everyone."

"Please everyone? As if you've tried! How about at least acknowledging the harm you caused?" Elise answered testily. "You have no idea of the ramifications, do you. I'm not just talking about the damage to police morale. I mean to me personally."

Vince exhaled deeply. "I'm more aware than you realize. My wife hit me with both barrels when she threw me out. Pressuring you to have an affair was ugly and arrogant. Anything else?"

Elise plowed ahead. "When I joined the force, a lot of guys harassed me because of my looks. Just when I started to feel like I'd won their respect, the chief, a man I trusted, treated me like some sleazy toy put there for his benefit."

Vince looked as if he'd like to argue. To Marta's relief, however, he gave a tight nod. "When you put it that way, I…well, I never considered how my actions affected you professionally," he conceded. "I figured the impact was on the personal level."

"Yeah, well, you ticked me off, but the worst part was that a lot of the guys assumed I must have done something to encourage you." Her voice shook with emotion. "After I filed my grievance, your buddies acted as if *I* were the one who'd betrayed my fellow officers. An attitude I'm sure you encouraged."

Marta braced for his denial. Instead, Vince replied,

"Probably, because I was full of myself and furious at having to take my medicine." His voice rasped in the quiet space.

To her credit, Elise didn't stop there, although Marta could tell the confrontation was painful for her. "I spent the past two years trying to regain the respect you stole from me. If not for a few people like Hale and Rachel and Joel, I'd have resigned. I've been so angry I've refused to let any guy near me. Well, I'm moving on."

"What do you want from me?" the older man asked.

"You've never apologized, not sincerely. You don't seem to have a clue why I'm angry!"

Ben, who'd obviously been listening, peered out of the playroom. "Yes, he does. He told me he acted like a jerk and that you had a right to be mad."

That surprised Marta. Elise, too, apparently. "Is that true?" she asked.

Vince shoved his hands into his pockets. "Yes. And for what it's worth, I truly am sorry."

Hardly a cathartic conclusion to all Elise had undergone, in Marta's opinion, and her friend indicated as much. "You're not *that* sorry. Not sorry enough to sacrifice anything."

"Like what?"

"Like volunteering elsewhere so I don't have to keep running into you." When he opened his mouth, she hurried on, "Don't give me that garbage about how much you love kids. You like being in the middle of things. Feeling important. Hobnobbing with Yolanda and posing as a good guy in front of the world. That's the real truth."

Vince opened and shut his mouth as if attempting to utter a rejoinder. What finally came out instead was: "Okay."

For a second, no one stirred. Then Ben said, "You can't quit!"

Vince gestured him to silence. "She's right. Saying I'm sorry is a far cry from demonstrating it. I caused Elise a lot of misery and now I'm annoying her on a weekly basis. She isn't out of line to insist that I suffer a little too."

"What about your students?" the young man demanded.

"The center gets plenty of volunteers." To Elise: "I'll tell Yolanda it's my decision. No reason to place any blame on you. And, Ben, I'd appreciate your keeping quiet about this."

"You shouldn't have to quit!"

"That's my decision," the man responded calmly. "Please don't repeat any of this."

"Whatever." Grumbling, the kid returned to the playroom and shut the door.

"You're truly going to resign?" Elise asked.

"Yes." He shrugged. "I'm still discovering how badly I messed up. Hope this helps. I'll sure miss the place."

After Vince went into the auditorium, presumably to talk to Yolanda, Elise stood staring in his wake. Then she turned and walked back into the storeroom. "Maybe he means it," she said.

Marta hadn't expected the ex-chief to fold, either. "He sounded sincere. How do you feel?"

"Deflated," the patrolwoman conceded. "I won. Shouldn't I be bouncing off the ceiling?"

"You'll feel better when he's actually gone." Marta returned to the books. She wanted to finish sorting before Derek returned.

Then Elise spoke again. "I'm calling it off. He can stay."

"Why?"

"I don't feel angry anymore," Elise explained. "And I appreciated his promising not to say why he's quitting. That was decent."

"You could sleep on this," Marta pointed out.

"I'd rather intervene before he goes too far. He'd better not expect us to be friends. I'm not *that* forgiving." Elise marched off.

Marta hoped her own tête-à-tête with Derek went equally well. She didn't hold out a lot of hope for that, though.

A quarter of an hour later, she heard the outer door open in the reception area and recognized his footsteps. Desperately, she wished they could start over. Begin again the night of their date.

If she'd suspected she might have a chance with him, she'd have proceeded more slowly. Had she let their relationship grow naturally instead of trying to cram a lifetime into one night, she might not be in this mess.

Too late. The scent of his aftershave teased at her. With luck, she would stumble on the right words to soften the blow.

That was the best she could hope for.

Chapter Twelve

Glittering strands of Christmas ornaments decorated the exterior of the whimsically named In a Pickle shopping center—so called because it occupied a former pickle-packing plant—and week-end buyers jammed the parking spaces. Derek almost regretted suggesting the mini-mall for their outing.

When he'd arrived at the center, he'd noticed the way Marta's shoulders sagged as she sat tidying stacks of books. Hoping to lighten her mood, he'd proposed the Caffeine Connection, a tea-and-coffee shop in the central court of the remodeled factory, and she'd consented. Her low energy, however, reawakened his concern for her well-being.

On the short drive, she'd perked up a bit as she described how Elise had faced down Vince and received an apology. Elise's subsequent willingness to forgive surprised Derek. "She's always seemed so hard-nosed."

"Must be Mike's influence." Marta broke off as they arrived at the Pickle. After several fruitless turns through the parking lot, Derek nabbed a spot when a vehicle exited in front of them.

Worth the hassle, he concluded once they reached the interior, which reminded him of a small village. Kiosks and boutiques, many featuring crafts or novelty items, opened onto wandering lanes. Soaps and scented candles perfumed the air.

When two children ran by, Derek rested one hand on

Marta's back, protecting her. He employed his greater bulk to ease through the knots of shoppers.

They passed Pickle Curios, one of Connie's shops. Marta paused to examine jars and cans of imported food.

"Rosa picks most of her own merchandise," she explained. "Connie gives us both a lot of leeway as managers. Anything we select that sells particularly well gets featured on the Web site, and we receive a small commission."

Derek lifted a container that, judging by the picture on the front, contained peppers. Labeled in Spanish, it bore the English words Product of Peru. "Rosa must hunt pretty far afield."

"She sure does." Marta indicated a llama-shaped piñata. "You can't find that at the big discount stores!"

A couple of shoppers were chatting in Spanish with Rosa Mercato, a sturdily built woman in her early forties. Apparently in response to their queries, she produced a brightly garbed doll that met with instant approval.

While ringing up the purchase, she waved to Marta. "Just the person I wanted to see! I'd like your opinion on a personal matter. Yours, too, Sergeant."

"Of course." He wondered why.

He found out when Rosa joined the two of them. "I need to ask about Mark Rohan," she explained.

She'd purchased a date with the traffic sergeant at the auction, Derek recalled. "What about him?"

She glanced toward the entrance. "I better talk fast before someone else comes in."

"Shoot," he said.

"We've been going out almost every night, and he's eager to get married. It's like a wild romantic fantasy, plus we'd both like kids, and if I don't have them soon—like tomorrow—I'll miss my chance." Rosa did indeed speak at a lightning pace, the words tumbling over each other. "But I'm afraid we'll wake up one morning and discover we made a horrible mistake."

Plenty of officers' marriages collapsed under the strain of

rotating shifts and cynicism, a by-product of observing the worst side of human nature day after day. "Police in general have a high divorce rate. Enjoy the fun while it lasts."

"Typical male!" Rosa's smile softened her scoff. "Marta?"

"Date for a couple more months and if you're still crazy about each other, get premarital counseling," was her response. "Then I'll dance at your wedding."

Rosa wavered. "He's six years younger than me."

"Nobody thinks twice if the *guy*'s that much older."

"Oh, yeah?" Derek teased. "I'm only four and a half years your senior and you consider me an antique."

Marta didn't so much as crack a smile. What *was* wrong with her?

Several customers entered. "Thanks, you two. I'll consider what you said." Rosa broke off to assist the new arrivals.

Derek guided his companion out of the store and through the throngs to the Caffeine Connection. Shiny green-and-red packages of coffee beans rimmed the counter, flanking a sign that touted them as stocking stuffers. Derek and Marta placed their orders and carried their drinks to a secluded table.

The clamor of voices and the tinkling of holiday music faded. "Must be an acoustical dead spot." Grateful for the break, Derek held a chair for Marta, although in Southern California guys rarely performed such gallantries.

She sank down, forgetting to thank him. That wasn't like her, either.

He barely managed to hold still as she stirred sweetener into her herbal tea and swallowed a sip. Finally he blurted, "What exactly did the doctor say?"

Large, frightened eyes met his gaze. "She…" The words seemed to get stuck. "This is awkward."

A new possibility occurred to him. "If you gave me a deadly disease, for heaven's sake just say so."

To Derek's astonishment, Marta burst out laughing. "What

an idea! I mean, that isn't funny, only… What I have definitely isn't contagious."

"Good." How bad could her condition be if she managed to chuckle about it? Yet she'd indicated she did have *something*.

Derek swallowed a sip of coffee, which turned out to be burning hot. He jerked instinctively and then, to his dismay, his right hand began to shake.

He prayed for the trembling to stop before it became obvious. Instead, the damn thing intensified until he knocked first his spoon and then the whole ceramic mug off the table.

It shattered, spewing hot liquid across the floor and his shoes. With a curse, Derek shoved his chair back from the table. At the jolt, Marta's cup skipped to the rim, where she barely rescued it from the same fate as his.

An employee hurried over. Marta apologized while shooting anxious looks in Derek's direction. He grabbed his wrist and tried to still the thing.

The palsy quit, finally. Too late to undo the damage, though. He'd created a scene, blown his composure and wrecked their date. That instant of humiliation had transformed the coffee shop and the mini-mall into a trap. Like a wounded animal, Derek required solitude.

"I have to drive you home," he said gruffly. "I'm sorry."

"Are you okay?" Marta asked.

"Yeah. Fine. First-rate." After trying to pay for the damage—the employee declined the offer—Derek escorted Marta to the car.

He wondered how much she'd observed. Suppose she described the incident to her friends? He ought to swear her to secrecy, but he couldn't do that without explaining.

The prospect provoked further irritation. He didn't even look at her as he steered toward her home. Mercifully, she didn't prod him or chatter. Her silence soothed his agitation slightly.

She'd revealed earlier that she'd walked to Villa Corazon, so he didn't have to drop her off at her car. Instead, he pulled in front of Marta's apartment building so off kilter he bumped the curb. As if his front-end alignment mattered, when his entire life had gone awry.

It might be about to spin off course completely. Because he saw no choice but to reveal the truth.

MARTA WAS PUZZLED by what had happened. One minute Derek was calmly inquiring about the doctor and then he'd started shaking. She'd been powerless to stem the resulting rage and couldn't figure out what, if anything, she'd done to provoke it.

Connie's joking accusation from years earlier rang in Marta's ears: "You assume that whatever goes wrong is your fault. You've elevated guilt to an art form." Yet this time, search for clues as she might, she didn't see any way in which she'd caused the problem.

The muscles in Derek's neck and jaw rippled with tension as he yanked on the parking brake. Afraid to speak, she opened the sedan door.

Although she'd expected him to leave her on the sidewalk, he joined her a moment later. They walked to her apartment without speaking.

The irony of the situation struck Marta: that after she'd overcome her reluctance to confide about the pregnancy, the meeting had dissolved for reasons beyond her control. And, at present, beyond her comprehension.

When they entered, her cherished little home felt too confined for the restless man who paced in behind her. Ordinarily, Marta might have attempted to soothe him. Today, she simply sank onto the couch and waited.

Derek stood facing her, arms folded. She noticed the stark masculine impact of the navy polo shirt stretched across his chest and the jeans sculpted to his long legs. She longed to touch him, but he was clearly in no temper to be soothed by her touch.

"I guess you saw my...embarrassing exhibition," he said tautly.

"Your hand shook." That had been the starting point, although it was his infuriated reaction that had created most of the awkwardness.

He plunged ahead. "I have Parkinson's disease, diagnosed about a year ago. That's why the department transferred me to public information. I'd rather no one else learned about this, please."

Stunned, Marta blurted, "I thought only old people..." She stopped, and wished she'd bitten her tongue before uttering those cruel words.

"That's what most people believe." Angrily, Derek began pacing. "In case you're curious, the cause is a mystery. And the course is unstoppable, which makes my future a big zero. Interesting life I've been leading, isn't it?"

She didn't have to ask why he'd kept this secret. Distress blazed from every movement. "That's why the auction worried you. You didn't want a crowd to see your symptoms."

Marta knew little about the disease. TV and newspaper images of sufferers flashed into her mind, except she wasn't certain which of many much-publicized afflictions she was picturing.

She might as well ask the tough questions. "How bad will it get? And how soon?"

"It's progressive," he responded. "Slow but inexorable. I'm taking medication to control the symptoms. Fate catches up with Sergeant Hit-and-Run, I suppose some people would say."

"Only if they're jerks!" she said. "I'm really sorry, Derek."

For anyone, the diagnosis would come as a blow. For such a fiercely independent man, the prospect of disability must seem intolerable.

"I don't want your pity," he ground out.

"That isn't pity." Marta sought a more accurate word. "It's

empathy. Don't forget that I understand what it's like to get the rug pulled out from beneath your feet. It happened to me."

Derek wavered, perhaps tantalizingly close to accepting that they were on the same side. Then the protective walls appeared to slam into place.

"I appreciate our similarities, but there's one fundamental difference. You can reclaim your future, and I applaud you for it. Mine's finished. This won't get better and it won't even stay the same." After nearly colliding with her TV, he glared at the thing before resuming his route. "I can hope for a medical breakthrough, but in the meantime, I have to live in the real world."

A world of bitterness and resentment. Under other circumstances, Marta might have remained silent rather than provoke him. But this strong, desirable man had no business sinking into despair.

"In the real world, you're still an incredible guy that any woman would value," she retorted. "Maybe that doesn't matter to you, but it ought to. As for your refusal to accept pity, what about *self*-pity? You're wallowing in that."

She stopped, shocked by her audacity. And by the fact that she'd just uttered the most scathing remarks of her life to the man she cherished.

Derek's eyes glittered with anger. "I suppose I should ignore the whole thing. Count my blessings, perhaps?"

Marta would never be sure what possessed her, but the next statement out of her mouth was: "Well, you'd better pull your act together, because you're about to become a father."

He froze. Disbelief displaced his wrath.

"That's why you visited the doctor?" he managed so say at last. "What about Thanksgiving Day?"

"I threw up," Marta explained. "Yolanda's pretty perceptive."

He seemed to be trying to assemble the pieces of a puzzle. "Did you already know?"

She shook her head. "I guess I was in denial."

Derek stared at the floor, breathing hard, as if he'd run all the way here. "What are you going to do?"

What was *she* going to do? Infuriating! How naive to have imagined that he might rise to the occasion by offering to help support her.

"It's yours as well as mine!" she snapped.

"I didn't mean to imply—"

"You implied that this is *my* problem and I should deal with it!" An inner voice warned her that she had passed into the realm of unfairness. In her current cranky state, she didn't care. "I'm sorry about your illness. That doesn't excuse you from shouldering the consequences of your actions! We *both* made love that night and neither of us stopped to use protection."

He stared as if she'd grown a second head. Marta doubted her friends would recognize her snappish self, either.

Derek responded at last with frustrating obliqueness. "What do you expect from me?"

She had no idea. Compassion and love weren't his style. "Nothing," she answered at last. "You've made it clear how you operate. Enjoy the moment and then throw out the baby with the bathwater. Literally, in this case."

He tried again. "Look, I'll do my duty."

That simple statement hurt more than an insult. "Please, don't spare a single second from your absorption in your own problems," Marta said angrily. "I survived the car crash without my father's assistance and I can survive this pregnancy without yours. I'm sure Connie and Rachel will be there for me, the way they always are."

"Marta…" He seemed at a loss for further words.

Maybe he expected her to function as usual, delving beneath the surface and empathizing until she drew out his deeper meaning. But the agreeable Marta had vanished. Blame her hormones, or maybe her heartbreak. No use pretending she didn't love the guy, for all his flaws. But this baby needed her more than he did.

"You'd better go." Pushing up from the sofa, Marta marched to the door and held it.

"This is getting to be a bad habit," Derek said with a hint of irony. "Throwing me out, I mean."

"I never did that before!"

"You tossed me out of your bed, didn't you?" His expression perplexed, he trudged toward the exit. "This conversation isn't over."

Hope, that eternal traitor, poked its head from the ashes of her dreams. Marta gave it a mental thump. "If you say so."

"We'll work this out. I wish…I meant for us to have fun on our date." Derek looked so lost, she nearly hugged him.

She had to stand tough or she'd fall apart.

No sooner had he vanished down the walkway than doubts assailed her. How could she have treated him with such coldness after he'd confessed his agonizing secret? Tough as he appeared on the outside, his behavior at the café had demonstrated his vulnerability.

The man had to cope with an incurable illness. Marta remembered his confession last week that he felt he wasn't contributing enough to the force. Guilt, depression and anger were all understandable responses.

Then she'd sprung the pregnancy on him. How unreasonable to expect him to counter with a romantic declaration!

Ashamed, she nearly dialed his number to apologize. If she caught him before he reached home, he might turn around and come back.

No. She wasn't ready for a rematch.

In the kitchen, Marta fixed a cup of herbal tea. Good thing she planned to dine with her two dearest friends tonight for the first time since her birthday. Although Connie usually spent Saturday evenings with her husband, Hale had flown to Lake Tahoe to go fishing with his father. As for Rachel's spouse, he'd volunteered to cover a hospital shift for the pediatric-emergency specialist.

Now that she'd told Derek about her condition, Marta felt free to enlighten Connie and Rachel. She longed for their comfort and uncritical companionship.

With an hour to spare, she logged on to the Internet and checked sites concerning Parkinson's disease. She'd better learn more before she ran into Derek again.

Phrases leaped out. "Cause unknown…possible genetic component…toxins in the environment…progressive impairment of neurons…a lack of the chemical messenger dopamine…" Technical, and scary.

The symptoms included tremors, slow movements, stiffness and balance problems. "Patients struggle to understand and control the disease," one author wrote. "Adapting is difficult."

What accusation had she flung at Derek? *Don't spare a single second from your absorption in your own problems.* She shuddered.

She switched off the computer, freshened her makeup and drove to the subdivision where Connie lived. Her ranch-style home lay next door to Hale's former dwelling. They still enjoyed his pool in good weather, and he and his pals played video games and drank beer in the den as in the old days, but Connie had mentioned that they planned to rent it soon.

When Marta rang the bell, childish giggles accompanied the thumping of little feet. Seven-year-old Skip admitted her, with five-year-old Lauren right behind.

"Hi, Marta!" the little boy greeted her. "We're having pizza!"

How could she have forgotten they'd be sharing the meal with two children? Cute as they were, the squirming and kicking under the kitchen table quickly wore thin in Marta's present frame of mind.

Connie kept too busy attending to the kids to register her cousin's unusual reserve. A relaxed Rachel grinned at odd moments as if relishing a private joke.

"What's up?" Marta asked after the kids finally dashed off to play with Lego in Skip's room.

"Two pieces of good news," the policewoman announced. "First, I made detective."

"Bravo!" Connie cheered.

"I didn't know you took the test!" Marta cried. "That's wonderful."

"Wasn't sure I wanted to leave patrol," Rachel conceded. "But Russ and I decided to add to our family. The second piece of news is, I'm pregnant!"

"Oh, my gosh! Oh, my gosh!" Connie ran around and hugged her.

Marta stammered out congratulations. Rachel required no encouragement to fill in the details, including a due date a month before Marta's.

Their babies would be almost the same age. They could grow up together. Or, she reflected with a pang, if she relinquished hers, she'd forever mark its stages of development by watching Rachel's child.

"Russ is beside himself," Rachel enthused. "He's crazy about kids anyway, and he missed Lauren's early years." Born out of wedlock, the little girl had been raised by her grandparents. Russ had only gained custody after their deaths, with his ex-girlfriend's consent.

"Hale suggested we provide Skip with a younger sibling one of these days," Connie noted. "Not too soon, though. I'm too busy with the Con Amore line. It's selling like hotcakes."

Marta listened with genuine gladness for her friends. Yet, much as she wished them well, she missed the old sense of riding—or sinking—in the same boat. Once, the three of them had shared everything. But since Rachel's and Connie's marriages, they'd entered a new stage of their lives.

She refused to dampen Rachel's high spirits by citing her own dilemma. So Marta smiled and held her problems for another day.

And as her friends celebrated plans for the baby, how she yearned to join Rachel in shopping for a stroller and a crib, in deciding on color schemes and choosing names. To keep this infant and treasure the marvelous changes as it grew.

Despite the sacrifice and the risk of further alienating Derek, Marta clung to a tiny spark of hope. And felt it growing like the baby nestled inside.

Chapter Thirteen

Late on Monday morning, Will Lyons's secretary, Lois, popped into Derek's office. Since her small office lay sandwiched between his and the chief's, she often put in an appearance instead of calling. "Hey, handsome. The boss wants to see you pronto."

"What's up?" Derek logged off the computer.

"Well, there's good news and bad news." Over the weekend, the sixtyish grandmother had obviously performed her monthly ritual of dyeing her hair. The color varied from carrot red to faintly pink; this time, it bore a lavender tint. "The good news is that Rachel McKenzie's pregnant, although I don't suppose he plans to discuss *that*."

Derek gave a slight start. "Good for her."

Interesting coincidence, or possibly an ironic twist by a fate that seemed determined to corner him. Since Marta's revelation on Saturday, he'd seen babies everywhere. In his condo complex. On television. At the supermarket. They aroused an unfamiliar tenderness coupled with near panic.

The responsibility of becoming a father threatened to overwhelm a future in which Derek might lose the ability to support himself, let alone a family. Furthermore, Marta's failure to appreciate the gravity of his illness had left him feeling isolated. He'd come to rely on her more than he'd realized.

"What's the bad news?" he asked.

Lois pursed her lips. "More trouble with Ben. Beyond that, I'd better not say."

"I understand." Derek accompanied her next door.

On Lois's desk stood a framed photo of her children and grandchildren, flanked by images of her nieces. She'd attempted on several occasions to matchmake for Derek, but had finally declared that his playboy reputation made him a bad bet.

With a quiet thanks, he went into the chief's sanctum.

Since assuming the role of media and community liaison, Derek routinely consulted with Will. No longer daunted by the large office with its conference table and multiple windows, he took his usual seat.

Lyons's brown hair looked uncharacteristically rumpled. "You'd better prepare for another PR mess. City council hired me to dry-clean our image, but my son keeps throwing dirt at it."

"What's he done now?"

"Last week I loaned him my personal car. He dropped it off first thing this morning, as agreed." The chief's thin mustache twitched. "Unfortunately, he also left a plastic bag with a trace of marijuana stuck in the crack of the passenger seat."

Stupid kid, Derek thought. Stupid to return to drugs and stupid to leave the evidence where his father would find it.

"With such a small amount, as you know, I have discretion about how to treat this. I keep asking myself, if he weren't my son, what would I do?" The words spilled out of the usually guarded man. "Even though I'd probably give a stranger's child a break, I'm not sure that's the right course in this case. I could smack that kid for putting me in this position!"

Derek recalled the open window he'd glimpsed in the parking lot. "Maybe someone else dropped it there."

Will dismissed the notion. "Don't try to excuse him. He's an expert at doing that already. I should have been tougher from the start. I left the discipline up to my wife, and after she died, I sympathized with what he must be going through. I was too soft. I missed the warning signs."

Ben had been fourteen when he lost his mother and seventeen when he got busted, Derek recalled hearing. "Drugs hook a lot of young people. You can't lay all the blame on yourself."

Regret shadowed the chief's eyes. "Who knows? My wife and I married young. Maybe we weren't ready. But he's a grown man now. He insists on living independently and claims to be an adult, so he ought to act like it."

Derek had never before related personally to the chief's situation. He certainly hadn't contemplated what kind of father he would become. Now the fact hit him that the baby-to-be inside Marta wasn't going to remain an infant. Whatever Derek chose to do, a young man or woman might one day hold him accountable.

"What's your decision?" He hoped the chief didn't intend to slap his son in jail.

"I'm not sure." Will stared through the window blinds. "I left a message on Ben's cell phone. Guess he's in class this morning. With luck, I'll calm down before he returns my call." Will thumped the desk. "I half believe he pulls stunts like this on purpose."

"If it's any consolation, I went through a troubled phase as a teenager," Derek said. "No drugs but some serious fighting. I grew out of it."

"Let's hope he does." The chief indicated Derek's notepad. "We'd better prepare a statement in case word leaks, which I have a nasty suspicion it will."

They spent the next half hour hashing out a declaration that summarized the events and the applicable law. Then Will left to attend a meeting with the city manager.

Derek ate a sandwich at his desk. With forty-five minutes left in his lunch hour, he decided to visit Marta. He'd intended to phone her and ask her to dinner, but his talk with the chief had provided new reason for him to take action.

He crossed to the hospital. In the lobby, through the glass wall of the boutique, he watched her assist two customers choosing a flower arrangement. Small and solicitous, she exuded patience as she produced balloons and cards for their selection.

Finally they completed their purchase and left. Derek entered the shop.

Marta's initial glint of warmth shaded into uncertainty. Their last encounter had obviously unsettled her.

Derek seized on a neutral opening. "I guess you've heard that Rachel's expecting."

"She told Connie and me yesterday. I didn't say anything about my situation yet." She halted, awaiting his reaction.

"About the last time we talked…" Derek cleared his throat. "I didn't conduct myself very well."

"I'm the one who screwed up," Marta replied. "I can't believe how insensitive I was. Derek, I've been reading about your illness. My comments were inexcusable."

"Hardly!" He'd said far worse to her. "Can you forgive *me* for the way I acted about the pregnancy?"

"I sprang it on you," she protested. "You must have been in shock."

"For once in my life, I'm apologizing. Enjoy the moment," Derek teased.

Her tension melted. If they hadn't stood in full public view, he had a feeling she'd be in his arms. Instead, they hovered a short distance apart.

"I'm glad you're not angry," Marta told him.

"Whatever course you choose, you have my support." Inadequate as that sounded, Derek considered it an improvement on his performance Saturday. "I can help with medical bills. Feed you hot tea and rub your feet."

Her tremulous smile touched him. "I'm having an ultrasound Wednesday afternoon. The doctor says I'm large for how far along I am. I'm betting it's because I'm so short and carrying a big guy's baby. Would you attend with me?"

"You mean we can see the baby already?" Matters were progressing faster than he'd expected. "Of course I'll go."

She beamed, a delightful sight to Derek. They set a time to meet on Wednesday and, after a little more discussion of Rachel's news, he headed back to work.

In front of the hospital, a young couple were tucking their infant into a car seat. Joy radiated from them. If only he had the capacity for pure, uncomplicated love, Derek thought. A chasm had always separated him from others, even before the Parkinson's struck.

He was waiting to cross Mesa View Boulevard when he saw two men on the steps of the police building. As broadchested Will Lyons faced the reedy figure of his son, their tense stances warned of an incipient explosion.

They'd picked far too public a site, in full view of the hospital as well as the detective bureau, which had windows on this side. Derek muttered imprecations at the traffic blocking his access.

Finally, the road was clear. As he approached, he heard Will snap, "If the bag wasn't yours, then whose? Who else rode in the car with you?"

Reluctantly: "Vince. But he didn't—"

"You allowed Vince Borrego in my car?"

"I didn't realize there were restrictions! I should have guessed you'd treat me like a child." Ben fisted his hands.

"Who's your dealer? Borrego?" Will challenged.

This quarrel had better move indoors, fast. "Chief," Derek said as he reached the sidewalk. "Why don't we—"

Ben ignored Derek. "Go ahead! Lock me up! You always like to throw your weight around. But don't blame a guy who's been more of a father to me than you ever will be!"

Flushing, Will grabbed his son's arm. The boy wrenched free and took a swing at his father. The blow glanced off his father's cheek, and then the two halted, stunned by their actions. Neither appeared to notice Tracy Johnson, who'd approached from outside Derek's range of vision with her camera lens trained on the scene.

Derek spotted her then and attempted to mount a defense. "This is a personal dispute between a father and son. I'm requesting that you respect their privacy."

She lowered the camera. "This is a public place, Sergeant, and the chief is a public figure."

Will descended on them, his expression grim. A red patch showed on one cheek.

Ben followed. "What's she doing here?" To Tracy: "You vulture! Why don't you leave us alone?"

"I'd be glad to print your side of the story." She switched on a small digital recorder. "Who do you think placed that marijuana in your father's car?"

"Get bent!" The boy stalked past her and vanished around the corner.

Obviously, her arrival was no coincidence. "Who told you about the drugs?" Derek demanded.

"I can't reveal my sources." She addressed the chief. "Are you going to turn the evidence over to the D.A.?"

The anger on Will's face alarmed Derek. Before his boss landed in further hot water, he interjected a paraphrase of their official statement.

"Under California law, possession of less than an ounce of marijuana constitutes a misdemeanor, as you ought to be aware, Miss Johnson. Considering that only a trace was present, the officer on the scene has discretion." Spontaneously, he added, "Furthermore, there's no proof someone didn't plant it as a prank, since Ben Lyons left the car parked at Villa Corazon with the window open."

Will shot Derek a startled glance. Tracy frowned. "Who told you that, Sergeant?"

"I observed it," he said. "Last Saturday. Now I have a question for you."

Her chin jutted. "Yes?"

"Who's tipping you off?"

"Like I said, I assure my sources of anonymity," she answered.

"Your source is using you to embarrass this department. Are you really content to be manipulated?" he pressed.

Tracy pocketed her recorder. "I'm not the one who got into a fistfight in front of half the town. And you confirmed the information about the marijuana. As long as my sources tell the truth, their motives are their business."

Derek and Will watched her walk away, then turned and entered the building. Neither spoke till they were inside the chief's office.

"What's this about an open window?" Lyons asked.

Derek regarded his boss apologetically. "I started to mention it earlier and got sidetracked."

"Was Vince around when you saw the open window? Never mind. Ben already admitted giving him a ride." The chief's fingers drummed his desk. "I guess anyone could have stuffed the thing into the seat crack."

"Something tells me you were intended to find it," Derek said.

"Who would do that? Other than Vince, of course."

Derek tried to recall which volunteers had connections to the police force, aside from Ben and Vince. Elise. Rachel and Connie. Also Ginger, the daughter of Lieutenant Justin Lindeman. Possibly other volunteers as well. "In a town this small, anyone could be involved."

"I'm afraid you're right." The weight of the world appeared to sit on the man's shoulders. "Besides, there's no excuse for my behavior a few minutes ago. I was returning from lunch when I ran into Ben. He acted truculent as usual, but that's no excuse. I'm supposed to be the responsible one, and I blew it."

"We're all human." Derek recalled his own overreaction in the coffee shop on Saturday.

"I'm not allowed to be, not in my official capacity." The chief sighed. "Maybe with further consideration Tracy

Johnson will decide a family quarrel qualifies more as gossip than front-page news."

After giving a noncommittal response, Derek returned to his duties. He doubted Tracy would back off, and tonight marked her deadline.

Although she must have been in the area to arrive so quickly, clearly someone had snitched. And Derek still had no clue to the traitor's identity.

MARTA HAD MIXED emotions about having the ultrasound. Flares of enthusiasm gripped her when she considered seeing her baby, yet she shrank from the hard choice ahead.

Her heart demanded that she keep the child. Her common sense warned against it.

She was helping an assistant unpack a set of stuffed toys half an hour before the appointment when Connie appeared. "I've been dying to see what these look like in the flesh, so to speak." She and Marta had viewed only Internet images before ordering the items. "Oh, gosh, they're darling!" She lifted a Christmas elf from the display rack. "Wish we'd bought more. I'm nearly cleaned out of novelties at the main store."

"We could place a rush order." The warehouse wasn't far.

"I'll call." Connie replaced the elf. "You keep glancing at the lobby. Expecting someone?"

"Yes." Marta pulled her aside. "I have a doctor's appointment."

"In the lobby?"

Might as well tell her. "No, an ultrasound. I'm pregnant."

Her cousin's mouth formed a silent *O*.

"It's all your fault," Marta added lightly. "You and your big fat birthday present."

Understanding dawned. "Derek's the father?"

Marta nodded.

"Have you told him?"

She pointed toward the hospital entrance, where he'd just put in an appearance. "He's going with me."

"And?" Connie inquired.

"And that's where matters stand," Marta concluded.

Her cousin grasped the point. "I'll butt out—for now. But if he does you dirt, I'm hiring a hit man."

"You could sic Hale on him," Marta suggested.

"They're too well matched. I'm not risking my husband's neck."

Connie greeted Derek with composure and sent them both on their way. To Marta's pleasure, Derek extended an elbow for her to hang on in the elevator en route to the radiology department, as if they were in this together.

And they were. For the moment.

Nora Dellums, the ultrasound technician, must have noticed Marta's name on the appointment sheet, but her eyes widened when Derek walked in. The woman quickly recovered her composure and proceeded smoothly.

By the end of the day, the entire staff would know that Sergeant Hit-and-Run had knocked up the gift-shop manager. Although Marta cringed, she appreciated Derek's willingness to reveal his paternity.

Changing into a hospital gown didn't strike her as a big deal until she had to lie down and expose her stomach. The combination of cold and nerves made her shaky.

Derek smoothed her hair reassuringly. Marta closed her eyes, relishing the contact.

The technician spread goop on her bare skin. As the scanning device tickled her abdomen, Marta studied the moving shapes on the monitor.

Derek stared raptly. "Is that the baby? It looks like a complete person, only incredibly tiny."

"That's the general idea," the technician answered.

He gave an embarrassed chuckle. "Wow, it's kicking up a storm! Can you feel that, Marta?"

"No. But it sure is cute." She could scarcely believe Derek's excitement.

"Now, this is interesting," Nora murmured.

Marta's gut clenched as she recalled the doctor's concern about her size. Was something amiss?

"Am I seeing what I think I'm seeing?" Derek inquired in a puzzled tone.

"Yup," the technician said. "Twins."

Twins? Incredible. Marta struggled to grasp the concept.

"Can you tell the gender?" Derek asked.

"Too early," Nora replied. "Sorry."

"They're sure active," Derek said. "I'm surprised she can't feel them."

"That's because they're tiny. Once they grow and get squeezed for space, she'll feel them all right." Nora snapped a photo through the device, which she shifted.

Derek remarked on the small beating hearts as Nora captured more images. Thank goodness no one expected Marta to talk.

Two insights struck her. The first was that she desperately wanted to hold these amazing creatures and watch them grow into adults.

The second was that if one baby posed a challenge, two presented an insurmountable obstacle. Without the aid of grandparents or a husband, she'd be cheating the children and herself.

No matter how much Derek enjoyed watching these little sweethearts, he gave no indication of being ready to take on such an awesome responsibility. The dream of keeping her children shrank inside Marta.

For the babies' sakes, she would have to give them up.

Chapter Fourteen

Derek couldn't stop stealing peeks at the shadowy shapes on the screen, certain he detected the curve of a nose or the thrust of an elbow. Two kids meant they might have a little girl like Marta and a little boy…well, hopefully with a sweeter temperament than his.

At the end of the session, the technician gave them each a photo of the twins to take home. "The babies' first pictures," she announced

Derek stared at his while Marta dressed. When she emerged, her forlorn expression tore at him.

"Let's get a cup of coffee—tea—in the cafeteria," he suggested. "You aren't ready to go back to work."

"Don't you have stuff to do?" she asked.

"Nothing urgent. Besides, I'd rather lie low." The atmosphere at the station had been tense since Monday's altercation.

"Did Joel attempt to talk to Tracy?" Marta was well aware of the situation.

"I didn't ask him to. I doubt very much he'd cooperate, and she wouldn't back off, anyway," Derek said.

Marta exited the elevator ahead of him. "I'm amazed they're still dating."

"Rumor has it she's taking tips from his ex-wife." The *Voice* office lay in the same strip mall as Connie's Curios. "That must help in handling him."

"Connie hasn't mentioned talking to her. Besides, Tracy's sharp enough to cope with Joel on her own."

When they reached the cafeteria, Marta accepted Derek's suggestion that she sit down and let him fetch the hot drinks. The staff had stuck glittery angels and red balls on an artificial Christmas tree in one corner, he observed. The place was nearly empty at this predinner hour and, despite the decorations, was rather stark.

When he set the lemon tea in front of her, Marta stared at it unhappily, although she'd requested that flavor. "I could bring you peppermint," Derek offered.

"Huh?" When she lifted her head, he saw tears brimming.

"What's wrong?" He felt a crazy urge to pull her onto his lap and soothe away her misery. "Did the ultrasound hurt, or is this one of those hormone things?"

She shook her head. "It's because I can't keep two babies."

Her words hit Derek hard. Foolishly, he'd begun picturing himself dropping in to visit Marta's place, watching the children grow and providing assistance. "What would you do?"

"Brian, the attorney who helped with Skip's adoption, probably knows some families," she said glumly.

He sought a compromise. "If you arrange an open adoption, we could stay in touch." He'd heard about mothers who managed to remain in contact that way.

She blew on her tea. "I think a clean break would be easier on everyone."

Derek glanced at the photo of two babies curled in eternal innocence. Hard to grasp that this might be as close as he'd ever come to holding them. "Do you have to decide now?"

"It *is* early in the pregnancy," Marta conceded. "Why?"

"I guess I'm not quite ready to say goodbye when we've only just said hello," he admitted.

She rested her chin on her palm. "Do you still want me to go home with you for Christmas? I'll probably be showing."

Derek didn't hesitate. "Absolutely."

"Talk about arousing curiosity!" Her face scrunched. "They'd *have* to ask questions."

"My family respects my space," he told her.

"But these are their grandchildren."

He hadn't considered that angle. His parents certainly doted on Minnie, and the prospect of two more babies would be hard for them to resist.

Well, he'd deal with that situation when it arose. The fact was that, for the first time in Derek's adult life, he actually looked forward to Christmas because he'd be sharing it with Marta. "The invitation stands."

"Okay." A tiny smile showed her relief.

His watch alarm sounded, and he swallowed his medication with the last of the coffee. The beep also reminded him to meet with a homeowners' group about forming a Neighborhood Watch, which meant he had to leave.

Marta declined his suggestion that she accompany him downstairs. "I'm having another cup."

Derek kissed her cheek. Although he wanted more contact, this was hardly the place. "Catch you later."

"You bet."

He took his photo of the twins with him.

CLOSING HER EYES, Marta relished the memory of Derek's eyes as he watched the ultrasound. That man possessed such depths of caring. He'd be a great dad if he broke through the emotional block that seemed to prevent him from enjoying a truly intimate relationship. Despite their friendship, she still didn't understand the foundation of that wall.

However, she refused to torture herself with wishful thinking. She knew Derek too well to be misled by his request that she delay a decision and by his desire to spend Christmas together.

She had to prepare for what lay ahead: giving up their babies, and ultimately losing Derek. Not to his illness—she could cope with that—but to his fundamental need to be alone.

After finishing her tea, Marta summoned the energy to return to the shop for the rest of the day, then drove home. Inside the apartment, she peered into her refrigerator with chagrin. She'd stocked two jars of pickles because of a craving, plus a bottle of milk and a couple of yogurts, but nothing that resembled dinner.

"There's always spaghetti," she said aloud, and was hauling out a pot when the doorbell rang. Puzzled, she opened the door.

"Chinese!" Connie held aloft a trio of take-out cartons.

"Ice cream!" Rachel displayed two half-gallon tubs.

"Best of all, we left the kids at home!" her cousin declared as they marched inside.

"Except the one in my tummy, which is very eager to meet your guy," Rachel added.

Marta should have realized Connie would tell Rachel about the pregnancy. They'd probably informed Hale and Russ, too. While Marta hoped the news didn't cause problems for Derek at work, she supposed the story would inevitably reach the police department.

"This is wonderful. Thanks, guys." She displayed the ultrasound picture. "Here's the latest scoop."

Connie squinted at it. "Am I seeing double?"

"Oh, my gosh, twins!" Rachel whooped.

They set the table and gathered around, discussing due dates and children and plans. The other two women listened sympathetically when Marta mentioned adoption, and to her relief, neither criticized Derek.

No judgments, no attempt to control her. And no need for either to state the obvious: that come what may, Marta could count on her friends.

THERE WERE A FEW DAYS in Derek's life that he wished he could have skipped. For instance, the day he landed in a knife fight with the high-school bully and got expelled. Also the day when the neurologist delivered the news about his illness.

The day following Marta's ultrasound fell into that category, too, for several reasons. First and least important, his sheer discomfort when he walked through the station to his office that morning and caught not only speculative looks but also Marta's name coupled with the word *pregnant*.

The only person to actually allude to the topic with him was Hale, who placed a coffee-shop latte on Derek's desk with the comment, "Sorry, no booze in there, but this oughta replace any vital fluids you lost." That was as far as the good-natured cop cared to venture.

The day's larger problem arrived in the form of the *Villazon Voice*. A shot of Ben landing a blow on Will's cheek dominated page one. Police Chief and Son, read the banner headline.

Although no one could blame Derek for failing to dissuade Tracy, he had the sense that he'd let the department down. Not only did his job call for riding herd on the media, but he also felt a personal responsibility to protect the chief.

The phone started ringing early and continued all day with requests for statements and interviews. A TV crew appeared in front of the station and when the chief declined to speak on air, posed two news personalities on the steps to reenact the scuffle.

Unable to reach Ben, Will requested that Derek contact Yolanda to find out if the press had invaded her property, as well. Yes, people had showed up, she replied, but Ben had left for class and would probably lie low afterward.

Elsewhere in town, an L.A. station broadcast from outside Vince's office, rehashing old scandals and confronting the former chief on his way to meet a client. Vince declined to comment on his successor's troubles.

December was a slow period for news, Derek supposed. Without elections to claim the public's attention and with the state legislature currently in recess, news shows had empty stretches to fill. Today, they were cramming them with annoying dispatches from Villazon.

As a countermeasure, Will agreed with Derek's recommendation to speak with a smattering of the more responsible newspapers and TV stations. That way, at least he had a chance to explain the situation in depth and apologize to the city for the indiscretion.

Derek monitored each interview, a precautionary measure that forced him to cancel his weekly hospital meeting. He missed dropping into the gift shop and wondered how Marta was feeling now about yesterday's discovery she was having twins. Considered inviting her for dinner tonight, but had to work late and settled for a meatball sandwich from Alessandro's Deli.

"The worst should be over," Derek told his boss as they decamped around 8:00 p.m. Even the hardiest reporters had gone home. "Tomorrow, let's hope they find some other target."

"You did a terrific job." The chief sounded drained.

"Glad to help." Derek wished he had Marta's talent for lifting burdens from other people's shoulders. Will could use bucking up, and the widower had no one to go home to.

Neither did Derek. Arriving at his condo, he sank onto the couch but left the TV off. Much as he normally enjoyed channel surfing, he refused to risk subjecting his nerves to a glimpse of a news show.

Sleep crept over him. When he awoke, he stumped upstairs. In his dazed state, the hall seemed ridiculously long and the rooms seemed hollow.

Two chunky toddlers raced toward him crying, "Pick me up, Daddy!" Behind them, Marta emerged from the bedroom, hair tousled and face alight. "Hi, honey."

He must be dreaming on his feet. Derek stripped off his clothes and climbed into bed. Although he'd intended to read, he was asleep in seconds.

HE'D THOUGHT Friday would mark an improvement.

It didn't.

The morning passed smoothly enough. As he'd predicted, the press had moved on to fresh pickings—overnight, the first heavy rains of the season briefly shut a couple of small airports and caused a mess on the freeways—and the chief spent the morning catching up on paperwork.

In midafternoon, Will slipped into Derek's office and shut the door. Although the chief occasionally stopped by with a comment or question, he rarely stayed. This time, he moved a stack of folders and dropped into a chair.

"What's up?" Derek asked.

"I want my meeting with you now to look completely casual," Will began. "Nothing of what we say gets repeated to anyone. That includes my secretary and Frank or any of the other captains."

"Okay." Puzzled, Derek waited for illumination.

"I want you to reserve the meeting space for a press conference Monday afternoon, if it's available." The police used the community room at the adjacent library for such events. "Tell the librarian we're holding a seminar. I'll inform the mayor and city manager Monday morning."

That statement rang ominously. "Inform them of what?"

"I've decided to resign."

A chill fell over Derek. In the past year and a half, he'd developed a deep respect for Lyons. The man might lack the easy fellowship that had made Vince popular during his term, but he possessed unshakeable integrity.

"You can't," Derek told him.

The chief managed a faint smile. "Is that your professional opinion?"

"It's my professional advice."

"The city hired me to solve its problems and instead I've created more. It's best I go before this snowballs," Will said gravely.

Derek wondered if a higher-up had applied pressure. "Is this solely your decision?"

"Yes. The city's been damn reasonable about the whole business. No one's pushing me."

Good. "You're a terrific chief and a decent man," Derek insisted. "Your departure will give the impression that you did something wrong."

"Believe me, I've considered the effect this will have on my career." Restlessly, Will shifted on the hard seat. "Forty isn't old enough to put out to pasture, but I have to consider my officers and my employers first."

Once the press got wind of this decision, retraction would only arouse further hubbub. Derek had to persuade him to reconsider now.

"This will hurt the department, not help it," he argued. "I'm convinced somebody's trying to undermine us from the inside. How else could Tracy have learned about the marijuana? It's probably an officer loyal to Borrego." He hoped by mentioning Vince to rouse the chief's fighting spirit. "Your resignation plays right into their hands."

"No matter who's behind this, they're damaging my relationship with my son. That alone is reason enough to quit," Will replied steadily. "And I'm at fault for allowing my personal problems to spill over into public view. I've drafted both a letter of resignation and a public statement, which I'd appreciate your editing."

Reluctantly, Derek accepted the papers the chief passed him. He wasn't ready to give up. "Let's put off the conference until Tuesday."

"Why?"

He didn't dare explain that he needed time to devise tactics. "For one thing, it's past Tracy's deadline," he improvised. "She's caused enough trouble. I think she deserves a bit of a tweak in return."

His logic amused the chief. "You have an admirably twisted mind, Sergeant. However, the longer we wait, the greater the chance of the news leaking."

"If neither you nor I talk to anyone, how can it?" A possible answer occurred to him. "By the way, have you swept for bugs?"

"Yes. With today's technology, though, a device can snoop from outside the building," the chief noted. "That was one of the reasons I chose to have this conversation in your office, although there's no guarantee of privacy anywhere."

Derek searched for a second reason to justify holding off. "Plus, the mayor and city manager might not like to feel pressured. Best to allow plenty of time to confer with them."

Will didn't look pleased, but finally he acquiesced. "I suppose you're right. Once I decide on a course of action, I'm eager to put it in motion, but you make excellent points. Thanks for the counsel. Wise as always."

"Adequate, anyway."

As Derek rose to shake hands, he hoped he got a whole lot wiser, fast. Because by Monday, he had to figure out a way to derail this entire misguided train.

Chapter Fifteen

Watching Derek bend over a book beside Tom gave Marta a thrill. Their first lesson, and already she could tell the boy was responding.

That Saturday morning, Derek had arrived at the homework center frowning, but the tension had evaporated as he immersed himself in the moment. He seemed to find this place as much of a refuge as the children did. He'd changed since their night together. Grown kinder and more open, in her opinion, and more sensitive to others.

Elise, however, chewed one fingernail distractedly while assisting a little girl with the alphabet. As soon as they completed their session, she hurried over to Marta.

"I could use an unbiased opinion," the patrolwoman admitted. "Do you mind?"

"Not at all." Having completed her own tutoring session, Marta had hoped to catch a few words with Derek, but across the auditorium he remained absorbed in conversation with Tom.

Since Elise requested privacy, they slipped out the back door. Across the alley lay tidy rear yards leading to small houses. Even in what might have been the dead of winter elsewhere, flowers edged the yards. The calla lilies and bird-of-paradise plants were particularly striking.

"It's Mike." The policewoman inhaled deeply. "We had a fight."

"That was bound to happen," Marta muttered without thinking.

A stunned gaze. "Why?"

"Because everything's been so darn perfect." She eased down onto the concrete steps, while her friend remained standing. "No relationship goes that easily."

"I wish I'd known!" Elise's kick sent a loose stone skittering across the cracked blacktop. "I cried all night."

Marta regretted her insensitive remark. "I'm sorry. What did you argue about?"

"Moving in together." The blond woman paused as a teenager whizzed by on a bicycle. She waited until they were alone again. "I suggested we rent a place together. He says he's not ready."

"You've been dating for less than two months," Marta pointed out.

"Having someone around who listens and understands— it's heavenly." Elise leaned against the building with a thump. "I assumed he was happy, too."

"Maybe he is, but not full-time. It can be draining to serve as someone else's sounding post." Marta spoke from experience. She'd had a few coworkers who exhausted her with their endless need for a sympathetic ear. "Plus, Mike fulfills the same function at work."

"That hadn't occurred to me," Elise responded slowly. "Should I stop confiding in him?"

"Not necessarily." Marta hadn't meant to imply that. "What does he get out of this arrangement? You should figure out how to meet *his* needs."

"I don't think he has any." A pucker formed between Elise's brows. "He's so *together*. Or maybe I'm not smart enough to figure him out."

"You don't have to be psychic," Marta assured her. "Just ask him what would make him happy. Then really listen to the answer."

Her friend groaned. "I've been selfish, huh?"

"I wouldn't say that. Surely you've explored his past and his feelings at least a little." She thought of Derek. Despite his reserved manner, he'd found out quite a bit about her, she realized.

"Mostly we discuss my issues," Elise conceded. "He makes all the arrangements, too. I'm going to insist on cooking dinner tonight instead of relying on him, and I'll encourage him to talk for a change."

"Don't rush it." For an adult, her friend lacked experience with men. Not that Marta had such a great track record herself. She supposed she'd benefited from watching Connie and Rachel struggle with their romantic problems. "Give him space. What's your hurry?"

"I'm afraid I'll lose him," Elise confessed. "Instead, I'm probably driving him off. Okay, slow and steady. Speaking of being selfish, I meant to wish you well with the pregnancy instead of rattling on about myself."

"Thanks." Marta answered a few questions and then said goodbye. Judging by Elise's swinging stride as she cut around the building to the parking lot, she was eager to implement her new plan with Mike.

Perched on the rear steps, Marta watched a couple of children play on a slide in one of the yards. She guessed their ages at about three and five. What would her babies look like as preschoolers?

The door opened behind her. From the corner of her eye, she glimpsed a tall, muscular figure in jeans and a black jersey.

Derek sat beside her. "You feeling okay?"

"I'm fine." She rested her cheek on his shoulder. His strong arm slid around her.

"You smell wonderful," Derek murmured. "A little different from usual, but nice."

"That's our new cucumber-mint shampoo," Marta replied. "Like it?"

He chuckled. "Didn't anyone ever teach you how to accept a compliment?"

"I must have missed that lesson. I guess the appropriate reply is thanks."

"You're welcome."

They sat for a couple of minutes, simply enjoying each other's company and the season-defying blooms across the alley. A poinsettia tree, probably a Christmas gift stuck into the ground years ago, splayed red blossoms beside a door, and a pink rosebush offered its last, brave flowers to the cool air.

"I have an idea I need to discuss and you're the only person I trust," Derek said abruptly.

Honored, Marta rested her arms on her knees. "Shoot."

"You can't mention this to a soul," he warned.

"Scout's honor."

In a low voice, he said, "The chief plans to resign on Monday and I've got to find a way to stop him."

Marta didn't have to ask for background because she'd seen the latest article in the *Voice*. She also understood Derek's loyalty to Will Lyons. "Any ideas how to accomplish that?"

"I'm going to smoke out the person who's tipping off Tracy." He stretched his legs. "Finding the worm in the apple won't undo the damage, but I'm hoping it'll persuade the chief to reconsider."

"Did he explain his reasons?"

"He blames himself for embarrassing the city, plus he's trying to protect what's left of his relationship with Ben."

Marta felt obligated to raise an awkward point. "Any possibility Ben's the source?"

Derek dismissed the notion. "The kid was horrified when Tracy showed up on Monday. And I don't peg him as a sneak. In fact, I have to bring him into the plan for it to work."

"What plan?" This ought to be interesting.

"I've decided to spread different rumors, one per suspect," he said. "If I hit my target, he'll call Tracy. Since Monday's her deadline, she'll phone me immediately to confirm."

"And you can tell who blabbed depending on which story she repeats." What an inspired scheme! "Have you selected your suspects?"

"Not entirely. I'd better do this right, because if I omit the culprit, the whole thing will fizzle." Derek rotated his shoulder as if to relieve a cramp. "The chief plans to inform the press on Tuesday. I won't get a second chance."

One candidate seemed obvious. "I'm guessing Vince made your list."

"Yep. But to be credible, the story will have to come from Ben, not me."

"I'm not sure he'll cooperate." The young man had been steadfastly loyal to the ex-chief.

"He might if I explain it correctly." Derek didn't elaborate.

"Who else made your list?"

"Our traffic lieutenant, Justin Lindeman. He's an old buddy of Vince's, and his daughter volunteers here." He explained his theory that someone had slipped the plastic bag into the chief's car at Villa Corazon.

Skepticism colored her reaction. "You can't believe Ginger would do that!"

"I don't exactly, but you have to admit she had the opportunity. Now, who did I omit?" Derek probed.

They discussed names and, after rejecting several, reluctantly decided on Joel. Although neither believed him to have intentionally betrayed his fellow officers, Tracy might have succeeded in teasing information out of him.

Derek had decided against involving more of Vince's allies in case some of them compared notes and detected the scheme. Also, he explained, "Dreaming up three rumors poses enough of a challenge."

Marta had a few ideas. Between the two of them, they finally came up with three credible stories.

One more problem occurred to her. "If you're wrong, eventually these guys will figure out you fed them lies. What then?"

Derek grimaced. "I'll take full responsibility, no matter what that entails. This is my plan, not the chief's. If there's a screwup, it's mine, too."

The implication dismayed Marta. "The department won't punish you, will it?"

"I'm potentially subjecting my fellow officers to further embarrassment in the press," he replied. "I can't even count how many rules I'm going to break. The bottom line is, I might have to leave."

Unthinkable for him to lose his job. "What would you do?" Marta asked.

"Since I can't manage real police work anymore, there's no question of applying to another city." His shoulders sagged. "My parents wanted me to go into accounting. Maybe I'm not too old to start over."

Crunching numbers might suit someone else, but not Derek. "No matter what happens, stick it out unless they fire you outright," Marta advised.

"If this blows up, it'll damage morale," he replied. "And if I tick off enough people, my ability to perform my job will suffer."

He sound defeated already. "The guys ganged up on Elise, remember? She weathered the storm and so will you."

Derek mulled over her words for a while. Then he said, "Let's go out tonight."

"Talk about dodging the issue!" Marta retorted.

"Yes or no?" he teased.

She nearly shouted her agreement. Then she remembered an insurmountable conflict. "I'm sorry. I promised to babysit for Rachel and Russ."

"Need help?"

He couldn't be serious! "I promised to help redecorate Lauren's dollhouse. Does that appeal to you?" Marta inquired.

"Afraid not." His mouth twisted ruefully. "Tomorrow night?"

"It's a date."

After agreeing on a time, they both rose a bit clumsily from the hard steps. They'd fallen into an easy camaraderie, Marta thought, an extension of the friendship formed at the hospital.

Sadly, she sensed that, once the babies were born, the wrenching process of relinquishment would inflict too much pain for them to continue. All the more reason to treasure this relationship while it lasted.

As DEREK HAD ANTICIPATED, Ben initially resisted. The two of them talked in the Villa Corazon center parking lot, leaning against the youth's battered compact.

Despite his promise to Will, Derek saw no alternative but to admit the real story. "Your dad intends to resign rather than keep dragging you through the wringer," he explained. "I'm asking you to help me identify the suspect by clearing the person your father blames—Borrego. When Tracy brings me some other tale, we can be certain she didn't hear it from Borrego."

Ben's irate expression boded ill. If he refused to cooperate or, worse, called Tracy with the truth, he could destroy the whole plan.

"I hate lying," he said.

"Don't you want to find out who framed you?" Seeking further ammunition, Derek added, "We still don't know who set fire to your apartment and planted drugs there. People assume that was part of Norm Kinsey's revenge scenario, but there's a strong possibility they're wrong." Kinsey had denied any knowledge of the fire shortly before dying of a heart attack.

"It certainly wasn't Vince!" the boy snapped.

"Then help me nail the real culprit."

Ben blew out an angry breath. "I gotta think about it."

"Now or never." Derek pressed home the point. "After this weekend, the guilty party escapes and your dad suffers a loss he doesn't deserve."

Unwillingly: "Yeah, okay. What should I say?"

Here came the hard part. "Tell him that although you didn't leave the weed in your father's car, he found out that you *did* smoke some at a friend's house. Now he insists on asking the D.A. to press charges." Derek braced for an outburst.

He got one. "Absolutely not! I'm clean!" More calmly, Ben appended, "I take regular drug tests at my pizza-delivery job, so I can prove it."

"Excellent. If he should repeat this nonsense to Tracy, we'll rebut it."

"He won't! And Vince'll be really disappointed about me supposedly smoking dope." Slowly, the young man concluded, "I guess he'll forgive me when I explain why I did this."

"He ought to appreciate your clearing him." Derek wouldn't bet on that, though. He still considered Vince the most likely instigator of the force's ongoing problems.

Ben lifted his chin. "When should I tell him?"

"Tomorrow—no later. And please don't talk to anyone else about this!"

"Okay."

Chalk up one of the three rumors, assuming Ben kept his word. Relieved, Derek strolled back into the building to retrieve his copy of the math textbook.

Today's tutoring session had gone well. With Tom cooperating, they'd worked through a couple of difficult concepts, and chatted later about events at school. Strange to recall that his original motive for volunteering had been to snoop. Despite the motive, he was happy he'd made the choice.

"Glad you're still here." Yolanda waved Derek into her office and opened her desk drawer. "I've been meaning to give you this." She handed him a plastic bag containing a man's watch. On closer inspection, he saw that the leather wristband was broken.

"Not mine, I'm afraid." He attempted to hand it back.

The older woman waved away the attempt. "I discovered it beneath a heap of old leaves while pruning my bushes. My dog, Furball, has a tendency to bury things, so I'm pretty sure he's responsible. However, I generally keep him on a leash."

Derek regarded her patiently. "I'm sure there's a reason you've brought this to my attention."

"The last time he got loose was last June, on the day of the fire." She let the significance sink in.

"So you speculate that the mystery man dropped it." As Derek recalled, Yolanda had reported glimpsing an adult male on the premises shortly before the blaze. She hadn't seen him clearly enough to give more than a general description. "I hate to be a spoiler, but there are lots of animals that could have buried the watch. A stray dog or a raccoon, for instance, or your pooch during a previous escape."

"Finding this jogged my memory," she replied calmly. "When I tried to catch Furball the day of the fire, he was carrying a shiny object. He got away, and I didn't catch him for another ten or fifteen minutes. With all the excitement, the matter flew out of my mind. If I'd thought about his treasure at all, I'd have assumed it was a piece of junk."

Derek took a closer look. An expensive-looking watch. Normally, one would expect the owner to notify Yolanda if he believed he'd lost it on her property. "Did you check with your neighbors?"

"No one's missing such an item." Briskly, she concluded, "Of course, one of the firefighters might have dropped it."

"I'll inquire." Derek tucked the plastic bag into his pocket to pass to Andie O'Reilly at the fire department. "There's always a chance it'll turn out to be important."

"I'd love for you folks to nail the culprit. Two people nearly died that day. And I spent months trying to collect the insurance and get the place repaired." More gently, Yolanda asked, "How are you and Marta getting along?"

"We're coping." That sounded abrupt, so Derek added, "She's a wonderful person."

"As are you." With that unexpected statement, she retrieved the phone from her pocket. "Vibrating," she noted, and answered the call.

Derek went to fetch the math book. Afterward, in daylight, he examined the watch again, hoping for a break—an inscription, perhaps. But it simply appeared to be a good-quality watch such as one might buy in any number of stores.

What might have been a lucky break didn't appear likely to save the day. His plan had better work, for his sake as well as the chief's.

By breaking his promise of secrecy and by deceiving other officers right down to one of his best friends, Derek was staking every chip he owned on a very long shot.

Chapter Sixteen

A police thriller might not be Marta's favorite type of movie, but she had to admit that Derek's choice proved entertaining. Afterward, they bought ice-cream cones at In a Pickle and sat on a bench inside the mall.

A perfect outing, until Derek said, "If this situation at work blows up in my face, I've decided to get the hell out of Dodge."

Something in Marta went bump. "Really?"

"Yeah. I always wanted to travel. My grandparents' influence, I guess," he explained. "I ought to do it while I'm still able."

She watched a couple sorting through embroidered pillows at a boutique across the corridor. "You mean a vacation?"

"I mean indefinitely. After you give birth, of course. If you're serious about adoption, you won't need me after that."

Marta's ice cream lost its flavor. Villazon without Derek. She couldn't imagine it. "Where—where would you go?" she stammered.

"Maybe Australia. Japan. China and Russia. Then on into Europe. One last hurrah." Derek shifted position to let a group of teenage girls saunter past. "Since the diagnosis, I've been hanging on to my savings, hiding out and waiting for decrepitude like an old man. I'd rather blow the whole wad, maybe sell my condo, instead. With real-estate prices so high, I could live on the revenue for ages."

"But you'd be alone!" She didn't dare say what she truly meant. *You can't leave. I'll always need you.*

"I function best alone." Perhaps to temper the harshness of his words, Derek said, "I feel better around you than with any other person I've met. But, Marta, I'm a dark soul and you're a bright spirit. I'd drain your happiness."

An insight struck her. "You don't believe anyone could really love you, do you?"

Done with his cone, he tossed the wrapper into a trash bin. "If they did, I'd kill their feelings day by day. Best to exit with panache."

"Coward," she accused.

He looked startled. "We all define courage differently, I guess."

She had no reply for that.

Derek changed the subject or, rather, returned to the topic that had obviously been on his mind: the attempt to smoke out Tracy's source. "I played pool with Joel last night, which seemed like the perfect opportunity to plant my story. I told him the chief is reopening the investigation into Vince's past activities to see if anything was overlooked."

Marta forced herself to refocus. "How'd he react?"

"He got a little annoyed. Basically, he thinks we should leave old scandals alone, a view I happen to agree with. It'll be interesting to see whether he repeats the tale to Ms. Johnson." Derek indicated her half-eaten cone. "Ready to go? You can finish that in the car."

"Lost my appetite." She disposed of the remnant, which was probably the only time in Marta's life she'd discarded ice cream.

At her apartment, she and Derek shared a long, sweet kiss marred by the aching knowledge that he might soon vanish from her world. The possibility of losing him to extensive travels hurt so much that Marta withdrew.

"You okay?" he asked when she stepped away

She attempted to cover her reaction. "Just my hormones wreaking havoc."

"I could run to the pharmacy," he offered.

"No, thanks. I'm tired, that's all."

Derek ruffled her hair and regarded her worriedly, but took her comment at face value. After a few more reassurances, he left.

Marta selected a novel to read and went into the bedroom. When her eyes continued to slide uselessly over the words, she leaned against the pillows and wondered whether anyone would ever break through the shell around Derek's heart.

The phone rang. She reached for it. "Hello?"

Her father's gravelly tone rasped through the wire. "Your aunt Anna tells me you're pregnant," he said without preamble. "Twins, according to her."

Amidst the recent turmoil, Marta hadn't considered that Connie might confide in her mother and that word would spread. "That's right," she confirmed. "Before you ask, I'm not married and don't plan to be."

She didn't mention the probability of adoption, because it was none of her dad's business. Harry Lawson had long ago severed any intimate connection between them.

"Being the last to learn about my grandchildren puts me in an embarrassing position," he grumped.

Instinctively, Marta started to apologize. But for what? "You shouldn't be surprised if I don't confide in you," she said.

A short silence greeted this bluntness. Then: "If you expect Bryn and me to pay your bills, you're barking up the wrong tree."

Her father's nerve astounded her. Marta's temper, already stretched thin, finally broke.

"You refused to help when the doctors told me not to work yet, so I got a job even though I ached constantly," she reminded him. "You didn't care that I had to drop out of college and couldn't become a teacher, but no thanks to you

I'm taking classes again. My expectations from you are what you've taught me to count on—a big fat nothing."

The outburst astonished her. She hadn't realized she'd held so much resentment.

"I'm sorry you feel that way." His voice dripped with disapproval.

Although she hadn't intended to open a breach, Marta refused to ease off. Instead, she concluded, "In case I don't see you before then, Merry Christmas. I'm sure I'll receive my usual gift."

Since her father didn't believe in giving presents to adult children, they'd ended when she turned eighteen. For a couple of seasons, Marta had baked him a holiday batch of his favorite cookies, but she'd quit after the accident.

"Merry Christmas," he muttered in response, and hung up.

How lucky that she planned to spend the holidays with Derek and his family, Marta mused. But no one could replace her parents.

She wished she knew how to bridge the gap. That responsibility, however, lay with the man who'd created it.

BY TEN O'CLOCK Monday morning, Tracy still hadn't contacted Derek. Apparently she'd heard neither of the rumors he'd spread so far.

He prepared to drop the last tall tale in Justin's ear. When he stopped by the traffic division, however, he found the lieutenant's office empty. As Derek turned to go, he ran into Sergeant Rohan.

Mark proudly announced his engagement to Rosa Mercato. "Some folks think we're rushing this, but you and Marta are two lengths ahead," he kidded. "Double trouble! Well done."

"Same to you." Derek added a few more congratulatory words before asking, "Any idea where Justin is?"

"He's at the dentist. Probably for another hour."

"Thanks."

Next stop: the detective bureau, since Derek routinely touched base with division leaders on Mondays. He hated it when the press blindsided him with inquiries about a development that hadn't made the morning report.

Captain Ferguson greeted him jovially. "I understand Marta reaped extra benefits from the bachelor auction. Picked out names yet?"

Derek framed a noncommittal answer. "We're still deciding." He moved on quickly. "Got anything for me?"

Frank cited a couple of twists in ongoing investigations. Nothing earthshaking. Derek was making notes when his watch beeped. Or at least he *thought* it was his watch. He looked up to see the captain tapping his own wrist. "I've got an appointment with a sales rep at the shooting range. Testing a new type of body armor the chief asked me to look into."

Frank's timepiece appeared similar to Derek's. "New watch?"

"Yep. You inspired me." Frank replaced the files he'd riffled through. "The alarm sure comes in handy."

"I know what you mean."

Something teased at the depths of Derek's mind. A new watch. *What happened to Frank's old one?*

Probably sheer coincidence. But a good detective, even a former one, didn't trust coincidences.

Before the captain could vanish out the door, Derek yielded to his gut instinct. "Has the chief talked to you yet?"

The older man paused. "Regarding?"

Out popped the story he'd prepared for Justin Lindeman. "He got some bad news from the doctor on Friday." A pretense of dismay. "Never mind. I shouldn't have said anything."

"What kind of bad news?" Frank pressed.

"Heart problem." Derek shrugged. "I discouraged him from issuing a press release. None of the public's business, and truthfully, I believe he needs to project an image of strength. Particularly now."

"The doctors can treat that stuff with medication these days," Frank said. "Let's hope he's okay."

"If he brings it up, act surprised." As if the chief were likely to mention a heart problem that didn't exist!

"You bet."

On the way to his office, Derek felt like kicking himself. He'd wasted his last rumor and lied to Will's right-hand man, to boot.

This threatened to be a very disappointing and possibly disastrous day.

MARTA'S FATHER called shortly before noon. "Bryn and I discussed what you said," he told her.

"You did?" Holding the cell phone to one ear, she peered through a blur of holiday ornaments toward the hospital's entrance, where a tall man had entered. Not Derek, to her disappointment.

"We're excited about becoming grandparents. Especially my wife. She regrets never having children."

Marta had assumed her stylish stepmother was childless by choice. "She does?"

"She married late and then…well, starting over as a father didn't interest me," Harry admitted. "I try to make her happy, but I'm no wiz at understanding women. Guess I don't have to tell you that."

The rueful tone was so unlike his usual curtness. "What exactly did you have in mind?" she asked cautiously.

He cleared his throat. "We'd like to set up a college fund for the children."

Marta supposed she ought to feel grateful. Under the circumstances, though, the sudden show of concern proved painful. "Dad, I can't keep these babies. Being a single mom with one child might be possible, but not two."

A slight tremor underscored his response. "This young man of yours isn't husband material?"

She sought diplomatic phrasing. "He has his share of problems."

"We might be able to...do more." Her father clearly struggled with the offer.

Marta's mood softened. "I appreciate that, Dad. But this is too big a responsibility for me to depend on you or Bryn. These children need a stable home and parents. I'm sorry."

"Me, too." With a sigh, he added, "Too little too late from me, huh?"

"Not too late to start being friends again," she suggested.

"How about we drop over on Christmas Eve? I've never visited your apartment." Although he and Bryn had made the twenty-mile drive from Irvine for Connie's wedding, they might have lived across the continent for all Marta saw of them.

"That would be wonderful."

She hung up in a better mood than before. A reconciliation just in time for Christmas would lift anyone's spirits.

DEREK ATE a sandwich at his desk and accidentally dribbled mustard on the chief's letter of resignation, which he was revising as slowly as possible. Well, it had to be printed out again, anyway, for Will's meeting with the mayor and city manager.

He'd invented a fourth rumor to spring on Justin, but the man had barely ducked into the building before departing for a meeting of the city traffic commission. Besides, with half his face numb, he'd been in no mood for chitchat.

Derek had to concede that he'd failed. His grand scheme had yielded zero results, and in the process he'd probably alienated a close friend as well as a superior.

Why had he bothered involving Frank? True, the man had applied for the chief's position two years ago, but he hadn't appeared to mind losing out. "Too much politics" had been his comment.

Also, the owner of the lost watch had likely set a near-fatal blaze. Derek couldn't picture the man he'd worked with for more than a decade as a criminal. He still hadn't transferred the watch to Andie's custody. Better take care of that now. With a baleful glare at the silent phone, he rose to his feet.

It rang.

"Hallelujah," he mumbled sarcastically, and answered. "Reed."

"This is Tracy Johnson" came the reply.

Derek nearly stopped breathing, until he reminded himself that she often called on Mondays. "What can I do for you?"

"According to the grapevine, the chief's got heart trouble. Care to comment?"

A chill ran through Derek. "So that's your source," he blurted. "Frank Ferguson."

Tracy coughed, but recovered fast. "You're free to speculate."

"It isn't speculation," he told her. "That story's a plant. As far as I know, the chief's healthy as a horse."

Tracy sputtered angrily. "I can't believe Lyons would stoop to this!"

"He didn't. Blame me." Before she could marshal a response, Derek went on the attack. "Frank's been playing you, Tracy. He's trying to force the chief to resign because he wants the job." That much had become obvious.

"His motives aren't my problem. I'm here to report the news."

Her attitude cracked Derek's polite veneer. "Off the record, there's a chance he planted that marijuana in the chief's car and torched Ben's place. Nice company you keep."

Then he hung up. Completely against policy to do that to a reporter.

Derek braced for another ring. Silence. He decided against sticking around. He'd better confess the whole story to his boss before Tracy reached him. At best, the truth might persuade the chief to stay and cost Frank Ferguson his job.

Unfortunately, it would probably also cost his own.

Chapter Seventeen

Marta fixed spaghetti for Derek Monday night and they ate in her small kitchen. He filled her in on the day's events, which she found fascinating yet also disheartening.

Frank had furiously denied everything, and thanks to his popularity, half the officers took his side. Although angry, Will had declined to suspend the captain simply for providing tips to the media.

He also hadn't fired Derek, but neither had he appreciated his subordinate's taking matters into his own hands. "I feel like I betrayed his trust, and he's been my strongest supporter. Aside from you," Derek added.

Despite the compliment, Marta wished there'd been a more satisfactory resolution. "He'll appreciate you more when he recovers from his shock. How did Joel react?"

"He's furious. Accused me of seeking to advance my career at other people's expense." A grimace. "I guess I'm about the most hated guy in the department at the moment. Lower than Frank."

"You did the right thing," Marta assured him. "Everyone ought to be grateful."

"At least it isn't all bad news." In the one bright spot, the chief had decided against resigning, pending the results of an investigation into the new evidence Yolanda had provided regarding the fire.

As for the recent discovery of marijuana, Will had filled in one damning detail. The morning Ben returned the car to Will, Frank reported a flat tire and requested a ride with Will to a city-related breakfast meeting he and Will were scheduled to attend. The captain had produced the bag, claiming to have sat on it.

"That sneak!" Marta snapped. "The chief ought to give you a medal."

"Yes, but I promised to keep his resignation a secret, and then I disclosed it to his son." Ruefully, Derek noted, "Also, Ben's trumpeting how this proves Vince's innocence, at least in connection with the leaks. You can imagine how well that goes over." When he raised his water glass, a slight tremor revealed his stress.

Marta posed the question that troubled her most. "What are you going to do now?"

"I haven't ruled out chucking the whole mess and stepping off the edge of the earth, figuratively speaking." Derek toyed with his salad. "However, I'll be damned if I'll leave while Frank's still posing as a victim. I'm seeing this through."

"Hooray!"

He smiled. "Enough about me. How're you?"

"You'll never believe what happened. My father the miser can't wait to be a grandpa." She related the story, omitting her announcement about the adoption, since Derek had asked her to postpone that decision.

Derek enjoyed the tale of transformation, she could tell. He cared about her, perhaps more than he realized. If she pushed a little harder—told him how much giving up these children was going to hurt, reminded him of the adorable little creatures they'd observed at the ultrasound—he might break down and marry her. The man hovered halfway to that point already.

But she refused to manipulate him. When she walked down the aisle, if she ever did, she wanted the man waiting at the altar to glow the way Hale had for Connie. She deserved no less.

Despite their closeness, Derek ultimately found refuge in

solitude. Until he freely gave it up, until he could cherish her and allow her to cherish him completely, she had to respect the gulf that separated them.

After dinner, they cuddled on the couch. Tangling together, touching and kissing seemed to lighten Derek's mood. If they hadn't both been concerned about the effect on the twins, Marta suspected they might have ended up in the bedroom. She decided to ask the doctor whether lovemaking posed a danger.

They parted at last, however, aware that both had to work the next day and Marta required extra sleep.

"Is there a chance Frank could escape repercussions?" she asked as he shrugged into his jacket.

"That depends. I believe this ends any chance of his ever becoming chief," Derek replied. "But whether he'll be charged with a crime remains to be seen. Meanwhile, I've made a bitter enemy."

"I'm on your side!" Marta told him.

Derek squeezed her gently. "That means more than you know."

When he was gone, Marta curled into bed imagining that he lay beside her. In her dreams, Derek held her all night.

'TWAS THE MORNING before Christmas, and all through the police department tongues were wagging. Fire marshal Gavin Light and investigator Andie O'Reilly had marched over from their offices next door and closeted themselves with the chief.

Derek struggled to focus on editing a press release about the success of the officers' bicycle project for needy kids. They'd collected thirty-seven new or refurbished bikes to distribute through local charities.

He hadn't heard from Tracy Johnson recently, although she always stopped by once a week to read the police log. She hadn't printed anything regarding Frank, who'd remained on the job in the two weeks since the revelation about his misconduct.

Many of Derek's fellow officers continued to treat him

with frosty civility. Joel's sarcastic remarks had, if anything, gained momentum.

A faint stir on the far side of Lois's office drew Derek's attention. The fire officials were departing.

His throat tightened. If the watch Yolanda had found proved a dead end, Frank's only offenses would be indiscretion and the likelihood—impossible to prosecute—that he'd planted the plastic bag to frame Ben.

The bad guys sometimes won. Every cop knew that.

Derek reread the press release, ran it through spell-check and e-mailed it to a list of newspapers, radio and TV stations. If he got lucky, maybe one or two would use it.

Lois's pink-topped head appeared in the doorway. "Chief. See. You." She grinned playfully. Good news or just holiday cheer?

"Thanks." Derek followed her.

Behind the oversize desk, Will sat with hands folded atop a report. He went straight to the point. "They found DNA on the watch that matches Frank's."

Finally a break, although far from conclusive. "Have they interrogated him?"

"He claims he lost the watch earlier." Will frowned. "Trusting fool that I was, I'd asked him to check on Ben's welfare because my son resented any interference on my part. Frank *had* visited the premises previously, as a favor to me."

"Which would explain how he knew Ben usually left the door unlocked," Derek said. "There's also Yolanda's sighting of a man about Frank's build, and her report of the dog carrying a shiny object the day of the fire."

"None of that proves he's an arsonist." Will tapped his blotter. "I'm going to suspend Frank while we present this information to the D.A.'s office. Whether or not they'll bring charges is another matter."

The guy might yet skate.

"I'm glad you're staying on permanently." Derek had

learned about that decision a few days earlier. "Sorry I disappointed you."

"Excuse me?" The chief shot him a startled glance.

"For breaking my promise and telling your son you planned to resign. And for going behind your back about Tracy."

"I never thanked you, did I." Will rubbed his jaw absently. "You've taken a lot of heat for what you did. The truth is, I'm damn grateful. You're one of this department's greatest assets."

The approval soothed Derek. He hadn't lost this man's respect, and that meant a lot more than the easy popularity with his colleagues. "Thanks. Happy holidays."

"Same to you." They shook hands.

The day's excitement hadn't ended. An hour later, Frank emerged from the chief's office in a rage. His insults and curses reverberated through the building.

Derek, buying a snack in the lunchroom, saw shock on the faces of the traffic sergeant and a dispatcher. Apparently they'd never guessed at the malice that lay beneath Frank's gregarious manner.

To avoid a possible confrontation, Derek stayed put until the captain had slammed out of the station. Robbery-homicide detective Jorge Alvarez ventured into the lunchroom for coffee.

"Man, I'm glad they confiscated his gun. I was afraid he'd go ballistic," he told Derek. "You were right about him."

"Yeah, he's a real hero." Joel materialized, dour as usual. "One more step in your rise to power, eh, Derek? Maybe you can leapfrog into the captain's chair and skip all that nonsense about testing for lieutenant."

Despite a frown, Jorge's only comment was an ironic "Merry Christmas, guys." He departed.

"I already told you I'm sorry for involving you," Derek responded. "I had to find out where Tracy was getting her scoop."

"And I look like a blabbermouth to you? Never mind. Mission accomplished—you're the chief's fair-haired boy now." Joel brushed past him.

Derek gave up. While he hated to see a friendship of many years' standing destroyed, the man refused to accept an apology.

At shift change in late afternoon, Rachel dropped into Derek's office. "Russ and I are holding an open house tomorrow afternoon. It'll run late so our friends can drop by after their shifts or family gatherings. You'll come, right?"

"Sure." His family's meals were held in the morning, with dinner at midday. "Is Joel attending? I'd hate to spoil your party."

"He'd better leave his attitude at home or Connie will tell him where to stick it." With a wave, she breezed out.

Christmas. Who could tell? Maybe some of the spirit would spill over in unexpected ways.

MARTA LIKED the Spanish colonial style of the Reeds' house in Costa Mesa. Two stories high with clean lines and a red tile roof, it sported a tasteful array of holiday lights that pierced the lingering overlay of morning fog.

"You grew up here?" she asked as she retrieved her shopping bag from the rear seat. Although Derek had insisted that gifts weren't necessary, she'd enjoyed choosing items from the boutique.

"We lived in an apartment when I was small." He collected his assortment of wrapped books. "We moved here when I entered school. Now, tell me how you chose items for people you've never met?"

"You mentioned that they enjoy chess, films and museums, plus there's a new grandchild. That gave me lots of ideas." Her choices included toys, a travel chess set, a calendar from a major museum and a box of all-occasion cards featuring scenes from classic movies.

"It sounds so easy. Not for me." Derek matched his pace to hers as they went up the walkway.

"The difference is that I enjoy picking out presents," she explained. "When something's a chore, you're bound to have trouble."

"That makes sense."

On the porch, he rang the bell. The door opened within seconds.

"Hi." A dark blond woman in her late fifties gave Derek a hug and introduced herself as Lainie. "We're delighted our son brought a friend."

Her gaze flicked over Marta's high-waisted green dress. She was either too polite or too stunned to inquire about the bulge.

"It was wonderful of you to invite me," Marta said simply.

In the vaulted living room, she met the rest of the clan: Derek's handsome father, Andrew; brother Thomas, an attorney in the county public defender's office; and sister Jill, an accountant who clearly doted on her four-month-old daughter, Minnie, and her husband, Aaron, a CPA.

Everyone greeted the new arrivals with cautious good cheer. Their wariness puzzled Marta.

Jill clarified the matter later as Marta helped her retrieve platters of hors d'oeuvres from the kitchen. "You must be good for Derek. He's in a friendly mood."

"What's he usually like?" Marta couldn't resist inquiring.

"Grumpy," his sister admitted. "We're all a little afraid of him, although I guess that's silly. When I was growing up, he seemed like this big angry brother who was always yelling."

Marta would have liked to learn more, but Lainie joined them and the subject changed. "Does your family live far away?" Derek's mother asked as she checked on the turkey.

"No, but my dad and stepmother go to her parents' home in San Diego." Happily, Marta added, "They dropped in last night, so we had a little celebration then."

She'd baked Harry's favorite cookies, which he'd greeted with surprise and pleasure. He and Bryn had given her a luxurious bathrobe, cherry-red like one that Marta had treasured as a child. The visit had been brief, but she hoped for more frequent contact in the future.

During the meal at the Reeds' house, conversation flowed

across the dinner table. Marta didn't talk as much as usual, partly so she could absorb more details about this family and partly to avoid accidentally mentioning Derek's illness or her pregnancy.

Afterward, everyone returned to the living room. With flames crackling in the fireplace, they opened presents, exclaiming over each. Then the adults joined in the Christmas carols, accompanied by Lainie's guitar.

Seated on the couch beside Marta, Derek laid an arm around her waist. Jill beamed and Derek's father gave a slight nod.

Marta liked these people, yet she sensed the truth of what Derek had told her: that he didn't quite fit in. While Derek helped his mother clear the coffee cups, the other three men discussed local politics. Jill came to sit with Marta.

"Derek is acting different today." The young mother dandled her baby. "He's actually enjoying himself. You guys should get married."

"I think so too." Quickly Marta murmured, "But don't tell him."

"I won't." The other woman sounded wistful. "I wouldn't dare. I've always wanted to get closer, but I've never known how."

That makes two of us. Out of respect for Derek, though, Marta held her tongue.

HIS BACK STIFFENED as he loaded the dishwasher. Derek tried in vain to repress the flash of pain, which must have shown on his face.

"You're young to have arthritis." His mother reached out to massage his muscles. She rarely touched him, Derek reflected as her fingers probed the tightness. "Have you seen a chiropractor?"

He couldn't summon the will for subterfuge. "It isn't arthritis, Mom. I have Parkinson's."

She stopped, out of sight behind him. "Derek, I'm so sorry.

My father had that. Don't you remember when you stayed with them in San Francisco?"

Derek searched his memory. Grandpa's use of a cane hadn't seemed remarkable. "I just thought he was old."

Lainie circled into view, her eyes glistening. "How long have you known?"

"About a year." He waited for the inevitable question about why he hadn't revealed his condition sooner.

Instead, his mother said, "And you kept it secret. Because that's the way we raised you, holding things inside."

"But you aren't like that with Jill and Tom." He placed one more glass in the top compartment and closed the dishwasher door.

As a teenager, he'd accused her of loving his siblings more. She'd always denied it. Now she replied, "You're right. Things were different with you that weren't your fault, Derek." Apparently uncomfortable at disclosing so much, she began snapping lids on food containers. "I adore your friend Marta. Are you—I mean, is she—is she pregnant?"

"Yes." To save his mother the trouble of inquiring, he said, "We don't plan on getting married."

"Why...why not?" Lainie asked hesitantly.

Had he really been so cranky with his mother that she expected a sharp retort to such a natural question? Abashed, Derek leaned against the counter. "Because I'm bad at relationships. Look at how cozy you and Dad are with the rest of the family. Even Aaron fits in better than I do. There's something wrong with me and I wouldn't wish that on Marta."

Tears shone on his mother's cheeks. "Oh, honey, there's nothing wrong with you. I should have told you sooner."

"Told me what?" He hadn't been prepared for the possibility of some long-held secret.

"Just a minute." She peered into the living room. "Good, they're all busy. Marta and Jill have hit it off. Derek, sit down."

As he complied, he remembered Marta's suggestion that

his birth might not have been planned. Okay, but his parents had obviously wanted kids, so what difference did that make?

Lainie perched opposite him. "Derek, you were an accident."

"I'd drawn that conclusion."

"Did you know we weren't married?" She sounded breathless.

That he hadn't guessed. "No."

She twisted her hands. "We were both in law school. While we'd discussed marriage, we'd left it up in the air. Then suddenly we had to decide."

Until Marta's pregnancy, Derek might not have understood. Now he pictured these two towering figures as uncertain kids. "Did you...consider giving me up?"

Tearfully, she conceded that they had. "In the end, I couldn't let you go. Dad came around, but I had to drop out of school. When you were two, I returned to school and he started clerking for a judge. We rarely got enough sleep, and we fought constantly. We even separated for a few weeks."

"Why did you get back together?" he asked.

"We missed each other."

He'd had no idea. "You should have told me."

"You were a baby! Later, we assumed we'd put everything behind us." She swallowed. "The possibility that our tensions affected you didn't occur to me. People used to say children are resilient. But I believe now that they're highly sensitive to emotion, negative as well as positive."

"Yet you had two more," he pointed out.

"Once I finished law school and Andy started earning decent money, things got better. We decided to complete our family with one more. Tom was an easy baby and your dad longed for a daughter, so..."

"So you had two little sweethearts and one curmudgeon." He couldn't hide the note of bitterness.

"Two compliant children and one with a forceful temperament." Lainie laid her hand on his arm. "Derek, I admire you tremendously. You have such strength and integrity. The qualities that drove me crazy in a toddler stand you in good stead as an adult. If I had to depend on one of my children in a crisis, I'd choose you."

He scarcely believed he'd heard correctly. "I don't deserve that. I've been nursing my adolescent resentment far too long."

"You have a right to be resentful. We should have seen a counselor, as my parents urged. Instead, when you erupted, we bailed out and sent you away." Lainie wiped a tear from her cheek. "A classmate of yours told me years later that you were fighting a bully that day to protect a younger child. When it happened, we simply accepted the school's description of you as a troublemaker. Derek, I'm so sorry."

She must have bottled up these regrets for ages. Like him, she hadn't known how to breach the gap.

From deep in memory drifted a comment Dr. Wrigley had made during her sessions with Derek. *Children who don't feel loved come to believe they're not lovable. They think they're flawed.*

His mother's words rang in his brain. *If I had to depend on one of my children in a crisis, I'd choose you.* He couldn't imagine a stronger declaration of love.

"Thank you for telling me this." Derek met her halfway for a big hug, not their usual tentative pat but an all-enveloping embrace. "I love you, Mom." His throat clogged.

"Be happy, son," she said. "That's all I ask."

Now he had to figure out how to do that.

Chapter Eighteen

Marta tried in vain to read Derek's expression on the drive back to Villazon. He'd been in a thoughtful mood since he and his mother disappeared into the kitchen. She gathered that he'd disclosed his illness, and had noticed a new rapport between the two of them.

His family had been warmer than she'd expected, and the memory of his sister's baby made her heart contract. Those people loved Derek, even if they didn't know how to reach him.

Right now, he seemed lost in reflection. Marta chose not to intrude.

Rachel and Russ lived at the end of a cul-de-sac in the Amber View development, on the east side of Villazon. Their front porch was ablaze with holiday lights.

When Russ welcomed them, they found about a dozen friends gathered in the living room. At a freestanding, carnival-style popcorn maker that scented the air deliciously, Rachel was filling yellow-and-red striped bags for the kids.

Greetings flew. As Marta returned them, she scanned the guests: Connie and Hale, Elise and Mike, detective Jorge Alvarez, Mark Rohan and Rosa Mercato—wearing an engagement ring—and Joel Simmons. No sign of Tracy. A large-screen TV showed a scene of snow falling across a woodland. That was as close as Southern Californians came to enjoying a white Christmas.

The chatter had died with their entrance. Connie broke the lull. "My mom says your cheapskate father bought you a bathrobe. I hope it has solid-gold buttons."

Marta settled onto the couch with a cup of hot apple cider. "It's a fresh beginning."

"Yeah, you can bet on Christmas to turn us all lovey-dovey," Joel grumbled.

Although Derek's forehead furrowed, he didn't reply. The others also let the comment slide.

The conversation ranged across topics from football games to, inevitably, Frank Ferguson's angry departure the previous day. "I'm sorry I missed it," Elise said. "He should have waited until shift change so more of us could hear."

"Yeah, and it was pretty thoughtless of the chief to duke it out with Ben during lunch hour," Hale joked. "A guy doesn't dare even leave for a sandwich. You don't know what you're going to miss."

Derek chuckled. Across from him, Joel looked away. But amid the ripple of laughter, Marta believed that humor had defused any tension. That is, until Mike innocently asked how the captain's position would be filled.

"Oh, they might pick one of us lieutenants, or just hand it to a bootlicker like Reed," Joel answered.

"Give it a rest!" Connie snapped.

Her ex-husband showed no sign of complying. "He should-n't mind. He's been angling for a promotion for the past year."

"I didn't ask to be community relations director," Derek replied calmly.

"You love it over there, kissing up to the chief. What happened to the guy who used to swear he'd never leave the field except in a pine box?" Joel demanded.

Sensing what came next, Marta gripped her cup tightly. Sure enough: "He got Parkinson's disease," Derek said.

In the abrupt silence, the children's voices echoed from down the hall. Playing a board game, Marta gathered.

"That's why the chief tapped you?" Hale asked at last.

Derek gave a short nod.

"Oh, hell." Joel sounded disgusted, but no doubt this time with himself. "I've been mad at Tracy for what she did to us, and I guess I took it out on you. Sorry, man."

"Apology accepted." Whatever Derek might have added was cut short when his phone rang. He excused himself to answer.

Marta watched his expression shift into duty mode. "Where?… Has anyone issued a statement?…I'm on it."

He clicked off. "There's been an explosion. I have to go deal with the media."

A chorus of questions greeted this disclosure. He responded that he had little information beyond the locale: Frank Ferguson's house.

That generated even more inquiries. He had no answers. "Watch the news channels. I'm sure you'll get a glimpse of my mug soon enough."

"We'll take Marta home," Connie volunteered.

"Thanks." Derek caught Marta's eye. "Walk me out?"

"Sure."

She accompanied him to the sidewalk. "Sorry I have to split." He lowered his head until their foreheads touched.

"I understand."

"Save New Year's Eve for me, will you?" he murmured.

"Of course." Marta sighed as he brushed a kiss along her temple. "Congratulations on telling everyone the truth. They needed to hear it."

"Yeah, I guess," he said. "I wish… Well, we'll talk later. Merry Christmas, sweetheart."

"Merry Christmas." She cherished the endearment.

Inside, the others pelted her with questions about Derek's illness. She answered as best she could.

"Nobody had a clue," Rachel observed when they'd exhausted Marta's knowledge. "Derek's always been such a tough guy. The kind who could deal with anything."

"Almost anything," she corrected.

Russ changed the TV station. A camera crew in front of Frank's home was running scenes of firefighters mopping up. The blackened garage, stark in the glare of spotlights, bore a gaping hole.

The group at Rachel's house stuck around until Derek appeared and issued a statement outlining the course of events. Earlier, several neighbors had reported a blast. Suspended police captain Frank Ferguson had been found dead after a bomb he was building accidentally detonated.

He'd left no indication of the bomb's intended target.

TRACY JOHNSON WAITED until the other reporters left, Derek noticed. This being a Tuesday, she didn't have to hurry.

She walked beside him as he trudged toward his car. "He meant to kill the chief, didn't he?"

"That's supposition," Derek responded automatically.

Despite his disgust with Ferguson, the man's horrific death twisted in his gut. Such a waste of a human life. He also found it hard to accept that his former colleague had plotted Will's murder.

"He must have been insane," Tracy said.

Yeah, maybe, Derek thought.

She stuck around while Derek unlocked the sedan. Something was still troubling her, he gathered.

"I have to respect my sources," Tracy told him. "But I'm responsible for what I choose to print, too."

"Next time, question the motives," he responded. "They matter. And they may guide you to a bigger story."

"I sure missed this one." Tracy tightened the belt on her red-and-green holiday-themed sweater. She must have been pulled from a celebration, too. "Joel underestimates you, Derek. You're not just a pretty face."

"All compliments gratefully accepted."

"Merry Christmas." She headed off, a solitary figure in the night.

He returned home, eager for a peaceful refuge. Tonight, though, the bare surfaces and neutral colors of the condo lost their appeal.

The condo needed updating. Next weekend, he'd see what he could do.

MARTA MISSED spending at least part of the following weekend with Derek. He had to help his sister with a project, he explained.

He kept busy at work during the week, too. The press descended daily for its fix of Frank-related scandals, she saw on the newscasts, as tales emerged of gambling debts, an ex-girlfriend threatening to bring abuse charges and a rambling pseudonymous blog that described the intention of destroying an enemy called "The Bogus Chief" with a car bomb.

His mental problems appeared to have kicked into high gear when Vince Borrego was forced to retire. Frank had assumed the position belonged to him by right. As his personality disintegrated, he'd blamed all his problems on the man he insisted had supplanted him.

In a positive development, Chief Lyons and his son reconciled. "It never occurred to me someone might try to kill my dad," Ben told an on-air interviewer. "I'd be lost without him."

Throughout the media frenzy, Derek's low-key manner provided a refreshing contrast. Marta only wished he could have accompanied her to a doctor's appointment on Monday, when Dr. Bennett decided to perform a second ultrasound as a safeguard.

All appeared well. This time the probe detected the babies' gender—both male.

Two boys. Two little Dereks. Marta ached to keep them so much she retreated to the ladies' room and cried for several minutes.

Then she washed her face and returned to her job, determined to maintain a cheerful facade. She refused to ruin this special New Year's Eve.

Derek collected her at seven. He looked, if possible, even handsomer than usual in a suit and dark shirt. "Would you mind if we swing by my place before dinner?" he asked. "I'd like your opinion on a new purchase."

"Okay." In the car, Marta tried to save her news for a more romantic moment, but it burst through her restraint. "I had another ultrasound. They're both boys."

"Is that for sure?"

"Apparently."

Aside from a blink, Derek showed no further reaction as he steered into traffic. Her spirits sank. Subconsciously, she realized, she'd hoped the news might affect him as strongly as it had her.

When they parked at his condo, memories rushed back— of that night before the auction, when she'd first experienced the full force of his attraction, and of their subsequent date, when tenderness had bloomed into a connection that would at some level bind them for the rest of their lives. Even if he refused to admit it.

"What's wrong?" Derek held the car door, waiting for her.

Marta struggled to contain a coil of emotions. Words sticking in her throat, she simply climbed out.

As they approached the entrance, Marta sought a light remark to disguise her feelings. Impossible. She loved him too much. They belonged with each other and with their children.

She halted on the front porch. He tried to reach past her with the key. "Let's go in. You'll catch a chill."

"I'm not cold." Marta cleared her throat. "I have to say something."

Derek arched one eyebrow. "Here? We're in full view of the street."

"Any reporters hanging around?" she asked.

"No, thank heaven. Planning to take a swing at me?"

"Not unless you tick me off." Marta summoned her courage. Once they entered his turf, she might lose her nerve. "I've always believed I had a duty to make others comfortable and happy."

"At which you've succeeded," Derek observed quietly.

"Maybe, but I also trained everyone, including myself, to ignore my needs. I'm not going to do that anymore," she said. "So listen up. If you don't marry me and keep these babies, Derek Reed, you're an idiot."

He stared at her for a moment. Then he asked dryly, "Is that a proposal?"

"I suppose so." Marta felt deflated. Was that the extent of his reaction?

Derek unlocked the door. "Let's continue this discussion inside."

When she entered, she gaped in surprise. The lights seemed brighter than she recalled, and the furniture had been shifted to clear space for a playpen. Safety netting covered the stair railing.

"Is your sister moving in?" She hoped his weekend project hadn't resulted from the breakup of Jill's marriage.

"No, although she did provide invaluable assistance," Derek murmured close to Marta's ear. "Let me show you the second floor."

In a daze, she let him guide her upward, past the window that overlooked glittering holiday decorations in the complex's central court. They passed the office, which now held exercise equipment along with a desk.

In the spare bedroom, the overhead dome illuminated a pair of cribs and a changing station, an animal-themed strip of wallpaper and matching curtains. "We settled on green and yellow. Too bad we didn't know the gender," he commented.

"We could have a girl later," Marta blurted, then blushed furiously.

"So you approve?" Derek asked.

She parroted his earlier words. "Is that a proposal?"

"Maybe we should draw straws to see which of us gets to say yes." He wrapped his arms around her. "I'll go first. Yes."

"Yes," Marta echoed.

A sigh escaped, as if he was releasing years of pent-up tension. "You were right," he said.

She relaxed against him. "About what?"

"I should have trusted my friends enough to tell them about my condition. And you were right that I'm still a real cop, too. I did the department a greater service by using my brain that I ever did with my muscles." He sank atop a sturdy toy chest and pulled her onto his lap.

"Is this strong enough to hold us?" she asked.

"Better be, because I suspect two little boys will be jumping up and down on it."

Sheer happiness enveloped her. Still, Marta remained practical. "How're we going to balance our careers and child rearing and all that?"

His teeth flashed a brilliant white. "Well, you can go to school full-time if you'd like. Later, I'll watch the kids at night and on weekends while you study or teach, and Hale speaks very highly of Vince's daughter's home day care. What do you think?"

"That's awesome," she admitted. "You've given this a lot of thought." She'd never expected Sergeant Hit-and-Run to turn into the kind of husband and father who stuck around.

He grew more serious. "Marta, I can't be sure what lies ahead. Physically, I mean. But the future doesn't seem so frightening if we're together."

As if anyone knew what the future held! She'd relinquished that illusion long ago. What mattered was the love they shared.

"To me, no matter what, you'll always remain the sexy man I fell in love with," Marta told him. "You're my best friend, too."

"Better than Connie and Rachel?" he teased.

"Better than the whole world."

He kissed her and they snuggled for a while. Then they went out to celebrate the new year.

The streets shone in the moonlight as they drove to the restaurant. Inside Marta, two little boys lay snug and safe.

Someday, she thought, she would tell them about this night and how it felt like a fairy tale. Except that, with Derek, the magic was real.

Silhouette®

Romantic
SUSPENSE

Sparked by Danger,
Fueled by Passion.

When evidence is found that Mallory Dawes
intends to sell the personal financial information
of government employees to "the Russian,"
OMEGA engages undercover agent Cutter Smith.
Tailing her all the way to France, Cutter is
fighting a growing attraction to Mallory while at
the same time having to determine her connection
to "the Russian." Is Mallory really the mouse in
this game of cat and mouse?

Look for

Stranded with a Spy

by *USA TODAY* bestselling author

Merline Lovelace

October 2007.

Also available October wherever you buy books:
BULLETPROOF MARRIAGE *(Mission: Impassioned)*
by Karen Whiddon
A HERO'S REDEMPTION *(Haven)* by Suzanne McMinn
TOUCHED BY FIRE by Elizabeth Sinclair

HARLEQUIN *Super Romance*

Welcome to our newest miniseries, about five
poker players and the women who love them!

Texas Hold'em

When it comes to love, the stakes are high

Beginning October 2007 with

THE BABY GAMBLE

by USA TODAY *bestselling author*

Tara Taylor Quinn

#1446

Desperate to have a baby, Annie Kincaid
turns to the only man she trusts, her ex-husband,
Blake Smith, and asks him to father her child.

Also watch for:

BETTING ON SANTA *by Debra Salonen* November 2007
GOING FOR BROKE *by Linda Style* December 2007
DEAL ME IN *by Cynthia Thomason* January 2008
TEXAS BLUFF *by Linda Warren* February 2008

Look for THE BABY GAMBLE *by* USA TODAY
bestselling author Tara Taylor Quinn.

Available October 2007 wherever you buy books.

There was only one man for the job—
an impossible-to-resist maverick
she knew she didn't dare fall for.

MAVERICK
(#1827)

BY *NEW YORK TIMES*
BESTSELLING AUTHOR
JOAN HOHL

"Will You Do It for One Million Dollars?"

Any other time, Tanner Wolfe would have balked at being
hired by a woman. Yet Brianna Stewart was desperate to
engage the infamous bounty hunter. The price was just
high enough to gain Tanner's interest…Brianna's beauty
definitely strong enough to keep it. But he wasn't about
to allow her to tag along on his mission. He worked
alone. Always had. Always would. However, he'd never
confronted a more determined client than Brianna. She
wasn't taking no for an answer—not about anything.

Perhaps a million-dollar bounty was not the only thing
this maverick was about to gain….

Look for MAVERICK

Available October 2007 wherever you buy books.

REQUEST YOUR FREE BOOKS!
2 FREE NOVELS PLUS 2
FREE GIFTS!

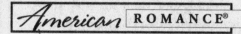

American **ROMANCE**®

Heart, Home & Happiness!

YES! Please send me 2 FREE Harlequin American Romance® novels and my 2 FREE gifts. After receiving them, if I don't wish to receive any more books, I can return the shipping statement marked "cancel." If I don't cancel, I will receive 4 brand-new novels every month and be billed just $4.24 per book in the U.S., or $4.99 per book in Canada, plus 25¢ shipping and handling per book and applicable taxes, if any*. That's a savings of close to 15% off the cover price! I understand that accepting the 2 free books and gifts places me under no obligation to buy anything. I can always return a shipment and cancel at any time. Even if I never buy another book from Harlequin, the two free books and gifts are mine to keep forever.

154 HDN EEZK   354 HDN EEZV

Name _____ (PLEASE PRINT)

Address _____ Apt. #

City _____ State/Prov. _____ Zip/Postal Code

Signature (if under 18, a parent or guardian must sign)

Mail to the **Harlequin Reader Service**®:
IN U.S.A.: P.O. Box 1867, Buffalo, NY 14240-1867
IN CANADA: P.O. Box 609, Fort Erie, Ontario L2A 5X3

Not valid to current Harlequin American Romance subscribers.

Want to try two free books from another line?
Call 1-800-873-8635 or visit www.morefreebooks.com.

* Terms and prices subject to change without notice. NY residents add applicable sales tax. Canadian residents will be charged applicable provincial taxes and GST. This offer is limited to one order per household. All orders subject to approval. Credit or debit balances in a customer's account(s) may be offset by any other outstanding balance owed by or to the customer. Please allow 4 to 6 weeks for delivery.

Your Privacy: Harlequin is committed to protecting your privacy. Our Privacy Policy is available online at www.eHarlequin.com or upon request from the Reader Service. From time to time we make our lists of customers available to reputable firms who may have a product or service of interest to you. If you would prefer we not share your name and address, please check here. ☐

HAR07

Harlequin® Historical
Historical Romantic Adventure!

A WESTERN WINTER WONDERLAND

with three fantastic stories
by
**Cheryl St.John,
Jenna Kernan
and Pam Crooks**

Don't miss these three
unforgettable stories about
the struggles of the Wild West
and the strong women who
find love and happiness
on Christmas Day.

Look for
A WESTERN WINTER
WONDERLAND

*Available October
wherever you buy books.*

Ria Sterling has the gift—or is it a curse?—
of seeing a person's future in his or her
photograph. Unfortunately, when detective
Carrick Jones brings her a missing person's
case, she glimpses his partner's ID—and
sees imminent murder. And when her vision
comes true, Ria becomes the prime suspect.
Carrick isn't convinced this beautiful woman
committed the crime...but does he believe
she has the special powers to solve it?

Look for

Seeing Is Believing

by

Kate Austin

Available October
wherever you buy books.

www.TheNextNovel.com

HARLEQUIN®

Mediterranean NIGHTS™

Sail aboard the luxurious Alexandra's Dream and experience glamour, romance, mystery and revenge!

Coming in October 2007...

AN AFFAIR TO REMEMBER

by
Karen Kendall

When Captain Nikolas Pappas first fell in love with Helena Stamos, he was a penniless deckhand and she was the daughter of a shipping magnate. But he's never forgiven himself for the way he left her—and fifteen years later, he's determined to win her back.

Though the attraction is still there, Helena is hesitant to get involved. Nick left her once...what's to stop him from doing it again?

HM38964

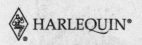

HARLEQUIN®

American ROMANCE®

COMING NEXT MONTH

#1181 THE RANCHER'S FAMILY THANKSGIVING
by Cathy Gillen Thacker
Texas Legacies: The Carrigans

Susie Carrigan and Tyler McCabe have always been friends—and sometimes lovers. Both fiercely independent, they've never been a couple, and never sought marriage. To anyone. But once Susie's matchmaking parents start setting her up on dates, Tyler starts thinking about their "friendship" differently. And wants those other guys to stay away from "his girl"!

#1182 MARRIAGE ON HER MIND by Cindi Myers

With a failed wedding behind her, Casey Jernigan arrives in eccentric Crested Butte, Colorado, ready for single life. But her landlord, Max Overbridge, could challenge that decision. His easygoing charm and his obvious interest are making her reconsider those wedding bells!

#1183 THE GOOD MOTHER by Shelley Galloway
Motherhood

Evie Ray and August Meyer were once high-school sweethearts. Now Evie's a single mom, doing her best to juggle work and motherhood, while August has taken over his parents' vacation resort. Seeing each other again, they realize there are still sparks between them. But will they be able to overcome past hurts to find love again?

#1184 FOR THE CHILDREN by Marin Thomas
Hearts of Appalachia

Self-reliant schoolteacher Jo Macpherson is on a mission to instill pride in the children of a Scotch-Irish clan living in Heather's Hollow, in Appalachia. She never expected to have to deal with intrepid Sullivan Mooreland, a far too appealing newspaperman who's on a mission to track down information about the Hollow that Jo has vowed not to reveal.

www.eHarlequin.com

HARCNM0907